MORE TISH

MORE WILDSIDE CLASSICS

MORE TISH

MARY ROBERTS RINEHART

WILDSIDE PRESS

MORE TISH

This edition published in 2006 by Wildside Press, LLC.
www.wildsidepress.com

THE CAVE ON THUNDER CLOUD

I

It is doubtful if Aggie and I would have known anything about Tish's plan had Aggie not seen the advertisement in the newspaper. She came to my house at once in violent excitement and with her bonnet over her ear, and gave me the newspaper clipping to read. It said:

> "Wanted: A small donkey. Must be gentle, female, and if possible answer to the name of Modestine. Address X 27, Morning News."

"Well," I said when I had read it, "did you insert the advertisement or do you propose to answer it?"

Aggie was preparing to take a drink of water, but, the water being cold and the weather warm, she was dabbing a little on her wrists first to avoid colic. She looked up at me in surprise.

"Do you mean to say, Lizzie," she demanded, "that you don't recognize that advertisement?"

"Modestine?" I reflected. "I've heard the name before somewhere. Didn't Tish have a cook once named Modestine?"

But it seemed that that was not it. Aggie sat down opposite me and took off her bonnet. Although it was only the first of May, the weather, as I have said, was very warm.

"To think," she said heavily, "that all the time while I was reading it aloud to her when she was laid up with neuralgia she was scheming and planning and never saying a word to me! Not that I would have gone; but I could have sent her mail to her, and at least have notified the authorities if she had disappeared."

"Reading what aloud to her — her mail?" I asked sharply.

"*Travels with a Donkey*," Aggie replied. "Stevenson's *Travels with a Donkey*. It isn't safe to read anything aloud to Tish any more. The older she gets the worse she is. She thinks that what any one else has done she can go and do. If she should read a book on poultry-farming she would think she could teach a young hen to lay an egg."

As Aggie spoke a number of things came back to me. I recalled that the Sunday before, in church, Tish had appeared absorbed and even more devout than usual, and had taken down the headings of the sermon on her missionary envelope; but that, on my leaning over to see if she had them correctly, she had whisked the paper away before I had had more than time to see the first heading. It had said "Rubber Heels."

Aggie was pacing the floor nervously, holding the empty glass.

"She's going on a walking tour with a donkey, that's what, Lizzie," she said, pausing before me. "I could see it sticking out all over her while I read that book. And if we go to her now and tax her with it she'll admit it. But if she says she is doing it to get thin don't you believe it."

That was all Aggie would say. She shut her lips and said she had come for my recipe for caramel custard. But when I put on my wraps and said I was going to Tish's she said she would come along.

Tish lives in an apartment, and she was not at home. Miss Swift, the seamstress, opened the door and stood in the doorway so we could not enter.

"I'm sorry, Miss Aggie and Miss Lizzie," she said, putting out her left elbow as Aggie tried to duck by her; "but she left positive orders to admit nobody. Of course if she had known you were coming — but she didn't."

"What are you making, Miss Letitia?" Aggie asked sweetly. "Summer clothes?"

"Yes. Some little thin things — it's getting so hot!"

"Humph! I see you are making them with an upholsterer's needle!" said Aggie, and marched down the hall with her head up.

I was quite bewildered. For even if Tish had decided on a walking tour I couldn't imagine what an upholsterer's needle had to do with it, unless she meant to upholster the donkey.

We got down to the entrance before Aggie spoke again. Then:

"What did I tell you?" she demanded. "That woman's making her a —"

But at that very instant there was a thud under our feet and something came "ping" through the floor not six inches from my toe, and lodged in the ceiling. Aggie and I stood looking up. It had made a small round hole over our heads, and a little cloud of plaster dust hung round it.

"Somebody shot at us!" declared Aggie, clutching my arm. "That was a bullet!"

I stooped down and felt the floor. There was a hole in it, and from somewhere below I thought I heard voices. It was not very comfortable, standing there on top of Heaven knows what; but we were divided between fear and outrage, and our indignation won. With hardly a word we went back to the rear staircase and so to the cellar. Halfway down the stairs both of us remembered the same thing — that it was Tish's day to use the basement laundry, and that perhaps —

Tish was not in the laundry, nor was Hannah, her maid. But Tish's blue-and-white dressing sacque was on the line, and the blue had run, as I had said it would when she bought it. In the furnace room beyond we heard voices, and Aggie opened the door.

Tish and Hannah were both there. They had not heard us.

"Nonsense!" Tish was saying. "If anybody had been hit we'd have heard a scream; or if they were killed we'd have heard 'em fall."

"I heard a sort of yell," said poor Hannah. "I don't like it, Miss Tish. The time before you just missed me."

"Why did you stick your arm out?" demanded Tish. "Now take that broomstick and we'll start again. Did you score that?"

"How'll I score it?" asked Hannah. "Hit or miss?" She went to the cellar wall and stood waiting, with a piece of charcoal in her hand. The whitewashed wall was marked with rows of X's and ciphers. The ciphers predominated.

"Mark it a miss."

"But I heard a yell —"

"Fiddle-de-dee! Are you ready?" Tish had lifted a small rifle into position and was standing, with her feet apart, pointing it at a white target hanging by a string from a rafter. As she gave the signal. Hannah sighed, and, picking up a broomhandle, started the target to swaying, pendulum fashion; Tish followed it with the gun.

I thought things had gone far enough, so I stepped into the cellar and spoke in ringing tones.

"Letitia Carberry!" I said sternly.

Tish pulled the trigger at that moment and the bullet went into the furnace pipe. It was absurd, of course, for Tish to blame me for it, but she turned on me in a rage.

"Look what you made me do!" she snapped. "Can't a person have a moment's privacy?"

"What I think you need," I retorted, "is six months' complete seclusion in a sanitarium."

"You nearly shot us in the upper hall," Aggie put in warmly.

"Well, as long as I didn't shoot you in the upper hall or any other place, I guess you needn't fuss," said Tish. "Ready, Hannah."

This time she shot Hannah in the broomhandle, and practically put her *hors de combat*; but the shot immediately after was what Tish triumphantly called a clean bull's-eye — that is, it hit the center of the target.

That is the time to stop, when one has made a bull's-eye in any sort of achievement, I take it. And Tish is nobody's fool. She took off her spectacles and wiped the perspiration and gunpowder streaks from her face. She was immediately in high good humor.

"Every unprotected female should know how to handle a weapon," she said oracularly, and, sitting down on the edge of the coal-bin, proceeded to swab out the gun with a wad of cotton on the end of a stick.

"The poker has been good enough for you for fifty years," I retorted. "And if you think you look sporty, or anything but idiotic, sitting there in a flowered kimono and swabbing out the throat of that gun —?"

Just then the janitor came down, and Tish gave him a dollar for the use of the cellar and did not mention the furnace pipe. Aggie and I glanced at each other. Tish's demoralization had begun. From that minute, to the long and entirely false story she told the red-bearded man in Thunder Cloud Glen several days later, she trod, as Aggie truthfully said, the downward path of mendacity, bringing up in the county jail and hysterics.

We went upstairs, Tish ahead and Aggie and I two flights behind, believing that Tish with an unloaded gun was a thousand times more dangerous than any outlaw with an entire arsenal loaded to the muzzle.

We had a cup of tea in Tish's parlor, but she kept us out of the bedroom, where we could hear Miss Swift running the sewing machine. Finally Aggie said out of a clear sky:

"Have you had any answers to your advertisement?"

Tish, who had been about to put a slice of lemon in her tea, put it in her mouth instead and stared at us both.

"What advertisement?"

"We know all about it, Tish," I said. "And if you think it proper for a woman of your age to go adventuring with only a donkey for company —"

"I've had worse!" Tish snapped. "And I'm not feeble yet, as far as my age goes. If I want to take a walking tour it's my affair, isn't it?"

"You can't walk with your bad knee," I objected. Tish sniffed.

"You're envious, that's what," she sneered. "While you are sitting at home, overeating and oversleeping and getting fat in mind and body, I shall be on the broad highway, walking between hedgerows of flowering — flowering — well, between hedgerows. While you sleep in stuffy, upholstered rooms I shall lie in woodland glades in my sleeping-bag and see overhead the constellation of — of what's its name. I shall talk to the birds and the birds will talk to me."

Sleeping-bag! That was what Aggie had meant that Miss Swift was making.

"What are you going to do when it rains?"

"It doesn't rain much in May. Anyhow, a friendly farmhouse and a glass of milk — even a barn —"

Aggie got up with the light of desperation in her eyes. Aggie hates woods and gnats, has no eye for Nature, and for almost half a century has pampered her body in a featherbed poultice, with the windows closed, until the first of June each year. Yet Aggie rose to the crisis.

"You shan't go alone, Tish," she said stoutly. "You'll forget to change your stockings when your feet are wet and you can't make a cup of coffee fit to drink. I'm going too."

Tish made a gesture of despair, but Aggie was determined. Tish glanced at me.

"Well?" she snapped. "We might as well make it a family excursion. Aren't you coming along, too, to look after Aggie?"

"Not at all," I observed calmly. "I'll have enough to do looking after myself. But I like the idea, and since you've invited me I'll come, of course."

At first I am afraid Tish was not particularly pleased. She said she had it all planned to make four miles an hour, or about forty miles a day; and that any one falling back would have to be left by the wayside. And that if we were not prepared to sleep on the ground, or were going to talk rheumatism every time she found a place to camp, she would thank us to remember that we had really asked ourselves.

But she grew more cheerful finally and seemed to be glad to talk over the details of the trip with somebody. She said it was a pity we had not had some practice with firearms, for we would each have to take a weapon, the mountains being full of outlaws, more than likely. Neither Aggie nor I could use a gun at all, but, as Tish observed, we could pot at trees and fenceposts along the road by way of practice.

When I suggested that the sight of three women of our age — we are all well on toward fifty; Aggie insists that she is younger than I am, but we were in the same infant class in Sunday-school — three women of our age "potting" at fences was hardly dignified, Tish merely shrugged her shoulders.

She asked us not to let Charlie Sands learn of the trip. He

would be sure to be fussy and want to send a man along, and that would spoil it all.

What with the secrecy, and the guns and everything, I dare say we were like a lot of small boys getting ready to run away out West and kill Indians. In fact, Tish said it reminded her of the time, years ago, when Charlie Sands and some other boys had run away, with all the carving knives and razors they could gather together, and were found a week later in a cave in the mountains twenty miles or so from town.

Tish showed us her sleeping-bag, which was felt outside and her old white fur rug within. Aggie planned hers immediately on the same lines, with her fur coat as a lining; but I had mine made of oilcloth outside, my rheumatism having warned me that we were going to have rain. I was right about the rain.

I had an old army revolver that had belonged to my father, and of course Tish had her coal-cellar rifle, but Aggie had nothing more dangerous than a bayonet from the Mexican War. This being too heavy to carry, and dull — being only possible as a weapon by bringing the handle down on one's opponent's head — Aggie was forced to buy a revolver.

The man in the shop tried to sell her a small pearl-handled one, but she would not look at it. She bought one of the sort that goes on shooting as long as one holds a finger on the trigger — a snub-nosed thing that looked as deadly as it was. She was in terror of it from the moment she got it home, and during most of the trip it was packed in excelsior, with the barrel stuffed with cotton, on Modestine's back.

Which brings me to Modestine.

Tish received three answers to her advertisement: One was a mule, one a piebald pony with a wicked eye, and the third was a donkey. It seemed that Stevenson had said that the pack animal of such a trip should be "cheap, small and hardy," and that a donkey best of all answered these requirements.

The donkey in question was, however, not a female. Tish was firm about this; but on no more donkeys being offered, she bought this one and called him Modestine anyhow. He was very dirty, and we paid a dollar extra to have him washed with soap powder, as our food was to be carried on his back. Also the day before we started I spent an hour or so on him with a fine comb, with gratifying results.

I must confess I entered on the adventure with a light heart. Tish had apparently given up all thought of the aeroplane; her automobile was being used by Charlie Sands; the weather was warm and sunny, and the orchards were in bloom. I had no pre-monition of danger. The adventure, reduced to its elements of canned food, alcohol lamp, sleeping-bags and toothbrushes, seemed no adventure at all, but a peaceful and pastoral excursion by three middle-aged women into green fields and pastures new.

We reckoned, however, without Aggie's missionary dime.

Aggie's church had sent each of its members a ten-cent piece, with instructions to invest it in some way and to return it multi-plied as much as possible in three months. This was on Aggie's mind, but we did not know it until later. Really, Aggie's missionary dime is the story. If she had done as she had planned at first and invested it in an egg, had hatched the egg in cotton wool on the shelf over her kitchen range and raised the chicken, eventually selling the chicken to herself for dinner at seventy-five cents, this story would never have been written.

What the dime really bought was a glass of jelly wrapped in a two-day-old newspaper. But to go back:

We were to start from Tish's at dawn on Tuesday morning. Modestine's former owner had agreed to bring him at that hour to the alley behind Tish's apartment. On Monday Aggie and I sent over what we felt we could not get along without, and about five we both arrived.

Tish was sitting on the floor, with luggage scattered all round her and heaped on the chairs and bed.

She looked up witheringly when we entered.

"You forgot your opera cloak, Lizzie," she said, "and Aggie has only sent five pairs of shoes!"

"I've got to have shoes," Aggie protested.

"If you've got to have five pairs of shoes, six white petticoats, summer underwear, intermediates and flannels, a bathrobe, six bath towels and a sunshade, not to mention other things, you want an elephant, not a donkey."

"Why do we have a donkey?" I asked. "Why don't we have a horse and buggy, and go like Christians?"

"Because you and Aggie wouldn't walk if we did," snapped Tish. "I know you both. You'd have rheumatism or a corn and you'd take your walking trip sitting. Besides, we may not always keep to the roads. I'd like to go up into the mountains."

Well, Tish was disagreeable, but right. As it turned out the donkey, being small, could only carry the sleeping-bags, our por-table stove and the provisions. We each were obliged to pack a suitcase and carry that.

We started at dawn the next day. Hannah came down to the

alley and didn't think much of Modestine. By the time he was loaded a small crowd had gathered, and when we finally started off, Tish ahead with Modestine's bridle over her arm and Aggie and I behind with our suitcases, a sort of cheer went up. It was, however, an orderly leave-taking, perhaps owing to the fact that Tish's rifle was packed in full view on Modestine's back.

I have a great admiration for Tish. She does not fear the pointing finger of scorn. She took the most direct route out of town, and by the time we had reached the outskirts we had a string of small boys behind us like the tail of a kite. When we reached the cemetery and sat down to rest they formed a circle round us and stared at us.

Tish looked at her watch. We had been an hour and twenty minutes going two miles!

II

We were terribly thirsty, but none of us cared to drink from the cemetery well; in fact, the question of water bothered us all that day. It was very warm, and after we left the suburban trolley-line, where motormen stopped the cars to look at us and people crowded to the porches to stare at us, the water question grew serious. Tish had studied sanitation, and at every farm we came to the well was improperly located. Generally it was immediately below the pigsty.

Luckily we had brought along some blackberry cordial, and we took a sip of that now and then. But the suitcases were heavy, and at eleven o'clock Aggie said the cordial had gone to her head and she could go no farther. Tish was furious.

"I told you how it would be!" she said. "For about forty years you haven't used your legs except to put shoes and stockings on. Of course they won't carry you."

"It isn't my feet, it's my head," Aggie sniffed. "If I had some water I'd b-be all right. If you're going to examine everything you drink with a microscope you might as well have stayed at home."

"I'd have died before I drank out of that last well," snapped Tish. "One could tell by looking at that woman that there are dead rats and things in the water."

"You are not so particular at home," Aggie asserted. "You use vinegar, don't you? And I'm sure it's full of wrigglers. You can see them when you hold the cruet to the light."

We got her to go on finally, and at the next well we boiled a pailful of water and made some tea. We found a grove beside the road and built a fire in our stove there, and while Modestine was grazing we sat and soaked our feet in a brook and looked for blisters. Tish calculated that as we had been walking for six hours we'd probably gone twenty-two miles. But I believe it was about eight.

While we drank our tea and ate the luncheon Hannah had put up we discussed our plans. Tish's original scheme had been to follow the donkey; but as he would not move without some one ahead, leading him, this was not feasible.

"We want to keep away from the beaten path," Tish said with a pickle in one hand and her cup in the other. "These days automobiles go everywhere. I'm in favor of heading straight for the mountain."

"I'm not," I said firmly. "Here in civilization we can find a barn on a rainy night."

"There are plenty of caves in the mountains," said Tish. "Besides, to get the real benefit of this we ought to sleep out, rain or shine. A gentle spring rain hurts no one."

We rested for two hours; it was very pleasant. Modestine ate all that was left of the luncheon, and Aggie took a nap with her head on her suitcase. If we had not had the suitcases we should have been quite contented. Tish, with her customary ability, solved that.

"We need only one suitcase," she declared. "We can leave the other two at this farmhouse and pack a few things for each of us in the one we take along. Then we can take turns carrying it."

Aggie wakened finally and was rather more docile about the suitcases than we had expected. Possibly she would have been more indignant; but her feet had swollen so while she had her shoes off that she could hardly get them on at all, and for the remainder of the day her mind was, you may say, in her feet.

At four we stopped again and made more tea. The road had begun to rise toward the hills and the farmhouses were fewer. Ahead of us loomed Thunder Cloud Mountain, with the Camel's Back to the right of it. The road led up the valley between.

It was hardly a road at all, being a grass-grown wagontrack with not a house in a mile. Aggie was glad of the grass, for she had taken off her shoes by that time and was carrying them slung over her shoulder on the end of her parasol. We were on the lower slope of the mountain when we heard the green automobile.

It was coming rapidly from behind us. Aggie had just time to sit on a bank — and her feet — before it came in sight. It was a long, low, bright-green car and there were four men in it. They were bent forward, looking ahead, except one man who sat so he could see behind him.

They came on us rather suddenly, and the man who was looking back yelled to us as they passed, but what with noise and dust I couldn't make out what he said. The next moment the machine flew ahead and out of sight among the trees.

"What did he say?" I asked. Aggie, who has a tendency to hay-fever, was sneezing in the dust.

"I don't know," returned Tish absently, staring after them. "Probably asked us if we wanted a ride. Lizzie, those men had guns!"

"Fiddlesticks!" I said.

"Guns!" repeated Tish firmly.

"Well, what of it? Our donkey has a gun."

And as at that instant the sleeping-bags and provisions slid gently round under Modestine's stomach, the green automobile and its occupants passed out of our minds for a while.

By the time we had got the things on Modestine's back again we were convinced he had been a mistake. He objected to standing still to be reloaded, and even with Tish at his head and Aggie at his tail he kept turning in a circle, and in fact finally kicked out at Aggie and stretched her in the road. Then, too, his back was not flat like a horse's. It went up to a sort of peak, and was about as handy to pack things on as the ridge-pole of a roof.

For an hour or so more we plodded on. Tish, who is an enthusiast about anything she does, kept pointing out wild flowers to us and talking about the unfortunates back in town under roofs. But I kept thinking of a broiled lamb chop with new potatoes, and my whole being revolted at the thought of supper out of a can.

At twilight we found a sort of recess in the valley, level and not too thickly wooded, and while Tish and I set up the stove and lighted a fire Aggie spread out the sleeping-bags and got supper ready. We had canned salmon and potato salad. We ate ravenously and then, taking off our shoes and our walking suits, and getting into our flannel kimonos and putting up our crimps — for we were determined not to lapse into slovenly personal habits — we were ready for the night.

Tish said there were all sorts of animals on Thunder Cloud, so we built a large fire to keep them away. Tish said this was the customary thing, being done in all the adventure books she had read.

Aggie had to be helped into her sleeping-bag, her fur coat having been rather skimp. But, once in, she said it was heavenly, and she was asleep almost immediately. Tish and I followed, and I found I had placed my bag over a stone. I was, however, too tired to get up.

I lay and looked at the stars twinkling above the treetops, and I felt sorry for people who had nothing better to look at than a wall-papered ceiling. Tish, next to me, was yawning.

"If there are snakes," she observed drowsily, "they are not poisonous — I should think. And, anyhow, no snake could strike through these heavy bags."

She went to sleep at once, but I lay there thinking of snakes for some time. Also I remembered that we'd forgotten to leave our weapons within reach, although, as far as that goes, I should not have slept a wink had Aggie had her Fourth-of-July celebration near at hand. Then I went to sleep. The last thing I remember was wishing we had brought a dog. Even a box of cigars would have been some protection — we could have lighted one and stuck it in the crotch of a tree, as if a man was mounting guard over the camp. This idea, of course, was not original. It was done first by Mr. Sherlock Holmes, the detective.

It must have been toward dawn that I roused, with a feeling that some one was looking down at me. The fire was very low and Aggie was sleeping with her mouth open. I got up on my elbow and stared round. There was nothing in sight, but through the trees I heard a rustling of leaves and the crackling of brushwood. Whatever it was it had gone. I turned over and before long went to sleep again.

At daylight I was roused by raindrops splashing on my face. I sat up hastily. Aggie was sleeping with the flap of her bag over her head, and Tish, under an umbrella, was sitting fully dressed on a log, poring over her road map. When I sat up she glanced over at me.

"I think I know where we are now, Lizzie," she said. "Thunder Cloud Mountain is on our left, and that hill there to the right is the Camel's Back. The road goes right up Thunder Cloud Glen."

I looked at the fire, which was out; at Modestine, standing meekly by the tree to which he was tied; at the raindrops bounding off Aggie's round and prostrate figure — and I rebelled. Every muscle was sore; it hurt me even to yawn.

"Letitia Carberry!" I said indignantly. "You don't mean to tell me that, rain or no rain, you are going on?"

"Certainly I am going on," said Tish, shutting her jaw. "You and Aggie needn't come. I'm sure you asked yourselves; I didn't."

Well, that was true, of course. I crawled out and, going over, prodded at Aggie with my foot.

"Aggie," I said, "it is raining and Tish is going on anyhow. Will you go on with her or start back home with me?"

But Aggie refused to do either. She was terribly stiff and she had slept near a bed of May-apple blossoms. In the twilight she had not noticed them, and they always bring her hay-fever.

"I'b goi'g to stay right here," she said firmly between sneezes. "You cad go back or forward or whatever you please; I shad't bove."

Tish was marking out a route on the road map by making holes with a hairpin, and now she got up and faced us.

"Very well," she said. "Then get your things out of the suitcase, which happens to be mine. Lizzie, the canned beans and the sardines are yours. Aggie, your potato salad is in those six screw-top jars. Come, Modestine."

She untied the beast and, leading him over, loaded her sleeping-bag and her share of the provisions on his back. She did not glance at us. At the last, when she was ready, she picked up her rifle and turned to us.

"I may not be back for a week or ten days," she said icily. "If I'm longer than two weeks you can start Charlie Sands out with a posse."

Charlie Sands is her nephew.

"Come, Modestine," said Tish again, and started along. It was raining briskly by that time, and thundering as if a storm was coming. Aggie broke down suddenly.

"Tish! Tish!" she wailed. "Oh, Lizzie, she'll never get back alive. Never! We've killed her."

"She's about killed us!" I snarled.

"She's coming back!"

Sure enough, Tish had turned and was stalking back in our direction.

"I ought to leave you where you are," she said disagreeably, "but it's going to storm. If you decide to be sensible, somewhere up the valley is the cave Charlie Sands hid in when he ran away. I think I can find it."

It was thundering louder now, and Aggie was giving a squeal with every peal. We were too far gone for pride. I helped her out of her sleeping-bag and we started after Tish and the donkey. The rain poured down on us. At every step torrents from Thunder Cloud and the Camel's Back soaked us. The wind howled up the ravine and the lightning played round the treetops.

We traveled for three hours in that downpour.

III

Only once did Tish speak, and then we could hardly hear her above the rush of water and the roar of the wind.

"There's one comfort," she said, wading along knee-deep in a torrent. "These spring rains give nobody cold."

An hour later she spoke again, but that was at the end of that journey.

"I don't believe this is the right valley after all," she said. "I don't see any cave." We stopped to take our bearings, as you may say, and as we stood there, looking up, I could have sworn that I saw a man with a gun peering down at us from a ledge far above. But the next moment he was gone, and neither Tish nor Aggie had seen him at all.

We found the cave soon after and climbed to it on our hands and knees, pulling Modestine up by his bridle. A more outrageous quartet it would have been impossible to find, or a more outraged one. Aggie let down her dress, which she had pinned round her waist, releasing about a quart of water from its folds, and stood looking about her with a sneer. "I don't think much of your cave," she said. "It's little and it's dirty."

"It's dry!" said Tish tartly.

"Why stop at all?" Aggie asked sarcastically. "Why not just have kept on? We couldn't get any wetter."

"Yes," I added, "between flowering hedgerows! And of course these spring rains give nobody cold!"

Tish did not say a word. She took off her shoes and her skirt, got her sleeping-bag off Modestine's back, and — went to bed with the worst attack of neuralgia she had ever had.

That was on Wednesday, late in the afternoon.

It rained for two days!

We built a fire out of the wood that was in the cave, and dried out our clothes, and heated stones to put against Tish's right eye, and brought in wet branches to dry against the time when we should need them. Aggie sneezed incessantly in the smoke, and Tish groaned in her corner. I was about crazy. On Thursday, when the edge of the neuralgia was gone, Tish promised to go home the moment the rain stopped and the roads dried. Aggie and I went to her together and implored her.

But, as it turned out, we did not go home for some days, and when we did —

By Thursday evening Tish was much better. She ate a little

potato salad and we sat round the fire, listening to her telling how they had found the runaways in this very cave.

"They had taken all the hatchets and kitchen knives they could find and started to hunt Indians," she was saying. "They got as far as this cave, and one evening about this time they were sitting round the fire like this when a black bear —"

We all heard it at the same moment. Something was scrambling and climbing up the mountainside to the cave. Tish had her rifle to her shoulder in a second, and Aggie shut her eyes. But it was not a bear that appeared at the mouth of the cave and stood blinking in the light. It was a young man!

"I beg your pardon," he said, peering into the firelight, "but — you don't happen to have a spare box of matches, do you?"

Tish lowered the rifle.

"Matches!" she said. "Why — er — certainly. Aggie, give the gentleman some matches."

The young man had edged into the cave by that time and we saw that he was limping and leaning on a stick. He looked round the cave approvingly at our three sleeping-bags in an orderly row, with our toilet things set out on a clean towel on a flat stone and a mirror hung above, and at our lantern on another stone, with magazines and books grouped round it. Aggie, finding some trailing arbutus just outside the cave that day, had got two or three empty salmon cans about filled with it, and the fur rug from Tish's sleeping-bag lay in front of the fire. The effect was really civilized.

"It looks like a drawing room," said the young man, with a long breath. "It's the first dry spot I've seen for two days, and it looks like Heaven to a lost soul."

"Where are you stopping?"

"I am not stopping. I am on a walking tour, or was until I hurt my leg."

"Don't you think you'd better wait until things dry up?"

"And starve?" he asked.

"The woods are full of nuts and berries," said Tish.

"Not in May."

"And there is plenty of game."

"Yes, if one has a weapon," he replied. "I lost my gun when I fell into Thunder Creek; in fact, I lost everything except my good name. What's that thing of Shakespeare's: 'Who steals my purse steals trash, . . . but he —'"

Aggie found the matches just then and gave him a box. He was almost pathetically grateful. Tish was still staring at him. To find on Thunder Cloud Mountain a young man who quoted Shakespeare and had lost everything but his good name — even Stevenson could hardly have had a more unusual adventure.

"What are you going to do with the matches?" she demanded as he limped to the cave mouth.

"Light a fire if I can find any wood dry enough to light. If I can't — Well, you remember the little match-seller in Hans Christian Andersen's story, who warmed her fingers with her own matches until they were all gone and she froze to death!"

Hans Christian Andersen and Shakespeare!

"Can't you find a cave?" asked Tish.

"I had a cave," he said, "but —"

"But what?"

"Three charming women found it while I was out on the mountainside. They needed the shelter more than I, and so —"

"What!" Tish exclaimed. "This is your cave?"

"Not at all; it is yours. The fact that I had been stopping in it gave me no right that I was not happy to waive."

"There was nothing of yours in it," Tish said suspiciously.

"As I have told you, I have lost everything but my good name and my sprained ankle. I had them both out with me when you —"

"We will leave immediately," said Tish. "Aggie, bring Modestine."

"Ladies, ladies!" cried the young man. "Would you make me more wretched than I already am? I assure you, if you leave I shall not come back. I should be too unhappy."

Well, nothing could have been fairer than his attitude. He wished us to stay on. But as he limped a step or two into the night Aggie turned on us both in a fury.

"That's it," she said. "Let him go, of course. So long as you are dry and comfortable it doesn't matter about him."

"Well, you are dry and comfortable too," snapped Tish. "What do you expect us to do?"

"Call him back. Let him sleep here by the fire. Give him something to eat; he looks starved. If you're afraid it isn't proper we can hang our kimonos up for curtains and make him a separate room."

But we did not need to call him. He had limped back and stood in the firelight again.

"You — you haven't seen anything of the bandits, have you?" he asked.

"Bandits!"

"Train robbers. I thought you had probably run across them."

All at once we remembered the green automobile and the four

men with guns. We told him about it and he nodded.

"That would be they," he said. As Tish remarked later, we knew from that instant that he was a gentleman. Even Charlie Sands would probably have said "them." "They got away very rapidly, and I dare say an automobile would be — Did one of them have a red beard?"

"Yes," we told him. "The one who called to us."

Well, he said that on Monday night an express car on the C. & L. Railroad had been held up. The pursuit had gone in another direction, but he was convinced from what we said that they were there in Thunder Cloud Glen!

As Tish said, the situation was changed if there were outlaws about. We were three defenseless women, and here was a man brought providentially to us! She asked him at once to join our party and look after us until we got to civilization again, or at least until the roads were dry enough to travel on.

"To look after you!" he said with a smile. "I, with a bad leg and no weapon!"

At that Aggie brought out her new revolver and gave it to him. He whistled when he looked at it. "Great Scott!" he said. "What a weapon for a woman! Why, you don't need any help. You could kill all the outlaws in the county at one loading!"

But finally he consented to take the revolver and even to accept the shelter of the cave for that night anyhow, although we had to beg him to do that. "How do you know I'll not get up in the night and take all your valuables and gallop away on your trusty steed before morning?" he asked.

"We'll take a chance," Tish said dryly. "In the first place, we have nothing more valuable than the portable stove; and in the second place, if you can make Modestine gallop you may have him."

It is curious, when I look back, to think how completely he won us all. He was young — not more than twenty-six, I think — and dressed for a walking tour, in knickerbockers, with a blue flannel shirt, heavy low shoes and a soft hat. His hands were quite white. He kept running them over his chin, which was bluish, as if a day or two's beard was bothering him.

We asked him if he was hungry, and he admitted that he could hardly remember when he had eaten. So we made him some tea and buttered toast, and opened and heated a can of baked beans. He ate them all.

"Good gracious," he said, with the last spoonful, "what a world it would be without women!"

At that he fell into a sort of study, looking at the fire, and we all saw that he looked sad again and rather forlorn.

"Yes," Tish said, "you're all ready enough to shout 'Beware of woman' until you are hungry or uncomfortable or hurt, and then you are all just little boys again, crying for somebody to kiss the bump."

"But when it is a woman who has given the — er — bump?" he asked.

Aggie is romantic. Years ago she was engaged to a Mr. Wiggins, a roofer, who met with an accident due to an icy roof. She leaned forward and looked at him with sympathy.

"That's it, is it?" she asked gently.

He tried to smile, but we could all see that he was suffering.

"Yes, that's it — partly at least," he said.

"That is, if it were not for a woman — " He stopped abruptly. "But why should I bother you with my troubles?"

We were curious, of course; but it is hardly good taste to ask a man to confide his heartaches. As Tish said, the best cure for a masculine heartache is to make the man comfortable. We did all we could. I dried his coat by the fire, and Tish made hot arnica compresses for his ankle, which was blue and swollen. I believe Aggie would gladly have sat by and held his hand, but he had crawled into his shell of reserve again and would not be coaxed out.

"I have a nephew about your age," Tish said when he objected to her bathing his ankle. "I'm doing for you what I should do for Charlie Sands under the same circumstances."

"Charlie Sands!" he said, and I was positive he started. But he said nothing, and we only remembered that later. We were glad to have a man about. Heaven only knows why women persist in regarding men as absolute protection against fire, burglars and lightning. But they do. A sharp storm came up at that time, and ordinarily Aggie would have been in her sleeping-bag, with Modestine's saddle on top by way of extra protection. But now, from sheer bravado, she went to the mouth of the cave and stood looking out at the lightning.

"Come and look at it, Tish!" she said.

"It's — Good gracious! There's a man across the valley with a gun!"

We all ran to the mouth of the cave except the walking-tour gentleman, who had his foot in a collapsible basin of arnica and hot water. But none of us saw Aggie's man.

When we went back: "Wouldn't it be better to darken things

up a bit?" he suggested. "If there are bandits round it isn't necessary to send out a welcome to them, you know."

This seemed only sensible. We put the fire out and sat in the warm darkness. And that was when our gentleman told us his story.

"Ladies," he began, "in saying that I am on a walking tour I am telling the truth, but only part of the truth. I am on a walking tour, but not for pleasure. To be frank, I — I am after the outlaws who robbed the express car on the C. & L. Railroad Monday night."

I heard Aggie gasp in the dark.

"Did you expect to capture them with a walking-stick?" Tish demanded. She might treat his ankle as she would treat Charlie Sands' ankle, but — Tish has not Aggie's confidence in people, or mine.

"Perfectly well taken," he said good-humoredly. "I left home with an entire arsenal in my knapsack, but, as I say, I lost everything when I fell into the flooded creek. Everything, that is, but my —"

"Good name?" Aggie suggested timidly.

"Determination. That I still have. Ladies, I'm not going back empty-handed."

"Then you are in the Government service?" Tish asked with more respect.

"Have you ever heard of George Muldoon, generally known as Felt-hat Muldoon?"

Had we? Weren't the papers full of him week after week? Wasn't it Muldoon who had brought back the communion service to my church, with nothing missing and only a dent in one of the silver pitchers? Hadn't he just sent up Tish's own Italian fruit dealer for writing blackhand letters? Wasn't he the best sheriff the county had ever had?

"Muldoon!" gasped Tish. "You Muldoon!"

"Not tonight or for the next two or three days. After that — Tonight, ladies, and for a day or two, why not adopt me to be your nephew — what was his name — Sands? — accompanying you on a walking tour?"

Adopt him! The great Muldoon! We'd have married him if he had said the word, name and all. We sat back and stared at him, open-mouthed. To think that he had come to us for help, and that in aiding him we were furthering the cause of justice!

He talked for quite a long time in the darkness, telling us of his adventures. He remembered perfectly about getting back the silver for the church, and about Tish's Italian, and then at last, finding us good listeners, he told about the girl.

"Is it — er — money?" Aggie breathlessly asked.

"Well — partly," he admitted. "I don't make much, of course."

"But with the rewards and all that?" asked Aggie, who'd been sitting forward with her mouth open.

"Rewards? Oh, well, of course I get something that way. But it isn't steady money. A chap can't very well go to a girl's father and tell him that, if somebody murders somebody else and escapes and he captures him, he can pay the rent and the grocery bill."

"Is she pretty?" asked Aggie.

"Beautiful!" His tone was ardent enough to please even Aggie.

He sat without speaking for a time, and none of us liked to interrupt him. Outside it had stopped raining, and the moon was coming up over the Camel's Back. We could hear Modestine stirring in the thicket and a watery ray of moonlight came into the cave and threw our shadows against the wall.

"If only," said Sheriff Muldoon thoughtfully — "If only I could get my hands on that chap with the red beard!"

We all went to bed soon after. Aggie, as usual, went to sleep at once, and soon, from, behind the kimono screen across the cave, loud noises told us that Mr. Muldoon also slept. It was then that Tish crept over and put her mouth to my ear.

"That may be Muldoon all right," she whispered. "But if it is he's got a wife and two children. Mrs. Muldoon is related to Hannah."

IV

Somehow, with the morning our suspicions, if we had any, vanished. Mr. Muldoon had been up at dawn, and when we wakened he had already brought water from a near-by spring and was boiling some in the teakettle.

Seen by daylight, he was very good-looking. He had blue eyes with black lashes and dark-brown hair, and a habit of getting up when any of us did that kept him on his feet most of the time. His limp was rather better — or his ankle.

"That's what a little mothering has done for me," he said gayly, over his coffee and mackerel. "It's a long time since I've had any one to do anything like that for me."

"But surely your wife — " began Tish. He started and changed color. We all saw it.

"My wife!"

"You've got a wife and two children, haven't you?"

He looked at us all and drew a long breath.

"Ladies," he said, "I see some of my painful history is known to you. May I ask — is it too much to beg — that — that we do not discuss that part of my life?"

Tish apologized at once. We could not tell, from what he said, whether he had been divorced or had lost them all from scarlet fever. Whichever it was, I must say he was not depressed for very long, although he had reason enough for depression, as we soon learned.

"It's like this," he said. "They know I'm here in the glen — the outlaws, I mean. The red-bearded man, Naysmith, has sworn to get me."

"Get you?" from Aggie.

"Shoot me. The other three all owe me grudges, too, but Naysmith's the worst. He's just out of the pen — I got him a ten-year sentence for this very thing, robbing an express car."

"Ten years!" I exclaimed. "You look as if you hadn't shaved in ten years!"

He looked at me and smiled.

"I'm older than you think," he said, "and, anyhow, he got a lot off for good behavior. It's outrageous, the discount that's given to a criminal for behaving himself. He got — I think I am right when I say — yes, he was sent up in '07 — he got seven years off his sentence."

We all thought that this was a grave mistake, and Tish, whose father was once warden of the penitentiary, observed that there was nothing like that in old times, and she would write to the governor about it. Tish has written to the governor several times, the last occasion being the rise in price of brooms.

"It's like this," said Mr. Muldoon. "They've got the glen guarded. There's a man at each end and the rest are covering the hilltops. A squirrel couldn't get out without their knowledge. I might have before I got this leg, but now I'm done for."

"Oh, no!" we chorused.

"It amounts to that," he said dejectedly. "They've been watching you women and they're not afraid of you. As long as I stay in the cave here I'm safe enough, but let me poke my nose out and I'm gone. It's an awful thing to have to hide behind a woman's petticoats!"

We could only silently sympathize.

It was bright and clear that day. The sun came out and dried the road below. It would have been a wonderful day to go on, but none of us thought of it. As Tish said, here was a chance to assist the law and a fellow being in peril of his life. Our place was there.

Even had we doubted Mr. Muldoon's story, we had proof of it before noon. A man with a gun came out on a ledge of rock across the valley and stood, with his hands to his eyes, peering across at our cave. Tish was hanging some of our clothing out to dry, and although she saw the outlaw as well as we did she did not flinch. After a time the man seemed satisfied and disappeared.

Tish came into the cave then and took a spoonful of black-berry cordial. As we knew, her intrepid spirit had not quailed; but, as she said, one's body is never as strong as one's soul. Her knees were shaking.

We put in a quiet and restful afternoon. Mr. Muldoon had a pack of cards with him and we played whist. He played a very fair game, but he was on the alert all the time. At every sound he started, and once or twice he slipped out into the thicket and searched the glen in every direction with his eyes.

He had asked us, if the outlaws surprised us, to say that he was Tish's nephew, Charlie Sands, and to stick to it. "Unless it's Naysmith," he said. "He knows me." From that to calling us Aunt Tish, Aunt Aggie and Aunt Lizzie was very easy. At four o'clock we stopped playing, with Mr. Muldoon easily the winner, and Aggie made fudge for everybody.

Late in the afternoon Tish called me aside. She said she did not want Mr. Muldoon to feel that he was a burden, but that we were almost out of provisions. We had expected to buy eggs, milk and bread at farmhouses, and instead we had been shut up in the cave. She thought there was a farm up the glen, having heard a cow-bell, and she wanted me to go and find out.

"Go yourself!" I said somewhat rudely. "If you want to be shot down in your tracks by outlaws, well and good. I don't."

Aggie, called aside, refused as firmly as I had. Tish stood and looked at us both with her lip curling.

"Very well," she said coldly; "I shall go. But if I get my neuralgia again from wading through the creek bottom don't blame me!"

She put on her overshoes and, taking a tin bucket for milk and her trusty rifle, she started while Mr. Muldoon was showing Aggie a new game of solitaire. I went to the cave mouth with her and listened to the crackling of twigs as she slid down into the valley. She came into view at the bottom much sooner than I had expected, having, as I learned later, slipped on a loose stone and rolled fully half the way down.

The next two hours seemed endless. Mr. Muldoon, tiring of

solitaire, had rolled himself up in a corner and was peacefully sleeping, with his injured foot on Aggie's hop pillow. Aggie and I sat on guard, one on each side of the cave mouth, and stared down at the valley, which was darkening rapidly.

Tish had been gone two hours and a half and no sign of her, when Aggie began to cry softly.

"She'll never come back!" she whimpered. "The outlaws have got her and killed her. Oh, Tish, Tish!"

"Why would they kill her?" I demanded. "Because she's trying to buy milk and eggs?"

"B-because she knows too much," Aggie wailed. "We've found their lair, that's why — don't tell me this isn't an outlaw's cave. It's just b-built for it. They'll do away with her and then they'll come after us."

Aggie never carries a secret weight in her bosom. She always opens up her heart to the nearest listener. This probably relieves Aggie, but it does not make her a cheerful companion. Eight o'clock and darkness came, and still no Tish. I went into the cave and brought out my gun, and Aggie roused Mr. Muldoon and explained the situation to him. He grew quite white.

"Good heavens!" he exclaimed. "What possessed her anyhow? To the farmhouse! Why, they'll —"

His face more than his words convinced us that the matter was really serious. He examined Aggie's revolver, which he mostly carried in his hip pocket, and, going to the mouth of the cave, listened carefully. Everything was quiet. The cave and both sides of the valley were in deep shadow, but over the ridge of the Camel's Back across from us there was still a streak of red sunset light. Mr. Muldoon looked and pointed.

Against the background of crimson cloud a man's figure stood out clearly. He was peering down toward us, although in the dusk he could hardly have seen us, and he carried a gun. Mr. Muldoon smiled faintly.

"Well, they've spotted me, I guess," he said. "I'd better move on before I get you into trouble. They won't hurt women."

"Why don't you shoot him?" Aggie asked. "It would be one bandit less. If you do arrest him, and he gets nearly all his sentence off for good behavior, he'll be out again in no time, doing more mischief."

But at that moment we saw the man on the hill throw his gun to his shoulder and aim at something moving below in the valley. Aggie screamed, and I believe I did also.

"Tish!" cried Aggie. "He's shooting at Tish!" And at that

instant the bandit fired. He fired three times, and the noise of his gun echoed backward and forward among the hills. We thought we heard a yell from, the valley. Then the next second there was a faint crack from below and the outlaw's gun flew out of his hands. Mr. Muldoon's jaw dropped. "Did you see that?" he said feebly. "Did — you — see — that — shot?"

The outlaw disappeared from the skyline and perhaps ten minutes later Tish crawled up to the cave and put down a tin pail full of milk, a glass of jelly wrapped in a newspaper, and a basket of eggs. Aggie fell on her and cried with joy.

"Be careful of those eggs," Tish warned her. "That outlaw charged me forty cents a dozen."

"You gave him a good fright anyhow," said Aggie fondly.

"Fright?"

"When you shot at him."

"Oh, that one! I'm talking about the woman at the farm."

"And — the one on the hill over there?"

"Oh! Well, he fired at me and I fired back. That's all."

With an air of exaggerated indifference Tish swaggered into the cave and took off her overshoes.

"Hurry up supper, Ag," she said — never before or since has she called Aggie "Ag" — "I'm starving."

She said she had heard little or nothing. She had found the farmhouse, had bought her supplies from a surly woman and had come away again. Asked by Mr. Muldoon if she had seen any men, she said she had seen a farmhand milking. That was all, except the outlaw on the hill.

But under her calmness Tish was terribly excited. I could tell it by her glittering eyes and the red spot in each cheek. Manlike, Mr. Muldoon did not see these signs; he ate very little and sat watching her, fascinated. Only once, however, did he broach the subject.

"I had no idea you were such a shot, Miss Letitia," he said. "It — that was a marvel."

"Oh, I shoot a little," said Tish coolly. "Only for my own amusement, of course."

Mr. Muldoon made no reply. He was very thoughtful all evening, did not care to play whist, and watched Tish whenever he could, furtively.

Tish herself was in an exalted mood, but not about the shot — she was modest enough about that.

And with cause. Months after she told us how it happened. She said she was carrying the eggs and milk with her left hand and had the gun in her right, when a shot struck a tree beside her. She was so startled that her finger pulled the trigger of her own rifle, which was pointed up, with the result we know of. She would probably never have confessed even then, had she not taken rheumatic fever and thought she was dying.

When Mr. Muldoon went out to fix Modestine for the night Tish called us to the back of the cave.

"I bought the milk and eggs," she said hurriedly, "and having a dime left — your missionary dime, Aggie, I borrowed it — I went back and bought a glass of jelly. Men like preserves. The woman wrapped it in a newspaper, and there is a full account of the robbery and of Muldoon being after the outlaws. He's after the outlaws, but he's after the reward too. They're quoted at a thousand dollars!"

"He can have the thousand dollars for all of me," said Aggie.

"A thousand dollars!" said Tish. "A thousand dollars to hand in to the church as the return from your missionary dime! And if we don't get it Muldoon will! As soon as he can get about on his leg he'll cease being hunted and begin to hunt. Why should he have it? He has plenty of chances, and we'll never have another."

That was all she had a chance to say, Muldoon joining us at that moment.

We retired early, but I did not sleep well. I wakened from time to time and I could hear Tish stirring next to me. At last I reached over and touched her.

"Can't you sleep?" I whispered.

"Don't want to," she whispered back. "I've got it all fixed, Lizzie. We'll take those outlaws back to the city, roped two by two."

It was a cool spring night, but I broke into a hot perspiration.

V

Tish began with Mr. Muldoon the next morning. He could not leave the cave to carry up water, for daylight revealed another guard across the valley and it was clear we were being watched. While Aggie and I went to the spring Tish talked to him.

She told him that he had undertaken too much, single-handed, and that he should have brought a posse with him. He agreed with her. He said he had started with a posse, but that they had split up. Also he insisted that but for his accident he could have managed easily.

"I'm up against it," he said, "and I know it. They'll get me yet. For the last day or two they've been closing up round this cave, and in a night or two they'll rush it. They've got their headquarters at that farmhouse."

"The thing for you to do then," said Tish, "is to get out while there is time. You can get help and come back."

"And leave you women here alone?"

"They're not after us," Tish replied, "and we've managed alone for a good many years. I guess we'll get along."

But when she proposed her plan, which was that he should put on Aggie's spare outfit and her sun veil and ride out of the valley on Modestine's back in daylight, he objected. He said no outlaw worthy of the name would fall for a thing like that, and he said he wouldn't wear skirts, and that was all there was to it.

But in the end Tish prevailed, as usual.

"I'm going to the farmhouse this morning and I am going to say that one of the ladies is leaving this afternoon and going back home. That will be you. I wish you had a razor, but the veil will hide that. They'll not molest you. You'll not only look like Aggie — you'll be Aggie."

Well, it seemed to be his best chance, although none of us dared to think what might happen if the hat blew off or Aggie's gray alpaca ripped at the seams.

We worked feverishly all day, letting out the dress and setting forward the buttons on her raincoat. Mr. Muldoon was inclined to be sulky. He sat at the back of the cave, playing solitaire and every now and then examining the road maps. Aggie was depressed too. But, as Tish said, getting rid of Muldoon was the first step toward the thousand dollars, and even if Aggie never got her gray alpaca again it had seen its best days.

That morning, while Aggie and I sewed and ripped and Mr. Muldoon sat back in the cave with the road map on his knees, Tish went to the farmhouse. She came back at eleven o'clock with a chicken for dinner and a flush on each cheek.

"I've fixed it, Mr. Muldoon," she said. "I talked to one of the outlaws!"

"What?" screeched Aggie.

"He'd come in for something to eat — the red-bearded one. We had quite a chat. I told him we were traveling like Stevenson — with a donkey; but that one of the ladies had an abscess on a tooth and was going home. He said it was no place for women and offered himself as an escort."

Mr. Muldoon groaned. "What am I going to do if one of them comes up and makes an ass of himself?" he demanded. "Kiss him?"

Tish looked at him coldly.

"You'll have your jaw tied up," she said. "That will cover your chin, and you needn't speak. Point to your jaw. Anyhow, they'll not bother you. I said the toothache had affected your disposition, and we were just as glad you were going. The red-haired man says he's got relatives near the mouth of the valley and you can stay there overnight. One of the men folks pulls teeth in emergencies."

It is hard, writing all this of Tish, to remember that she has always been a truthful woman. As Charlie Sands said later, when we told him the story and he had sat, open-mouthed, staring from one to the other of us, no one knows what depths of mendacity lie behind the most virtuous countenance.

We started "Aggie" off at two o'clock that afternoon, sitting sideways on Modestine, jaw tied up, veiled and sun-hatted, with Aggie's flowered-silk bag hanging to one wrist and a lunch-basket on the other arm. Tish and I saw "her" down the hill and kissed "her" good-by.

This was Tish's idea. I thought it unnecessary, but as a matter of fact, no matter what Charlie Sands may say, it was not a real kiss, going as it did through a veil and a bandage.

The man with a gun watched "her" off, and Tish, having waved "her" out of sight round a curve, looked up at him and nodded. Far away as he was, he saw that and swept his hat off with quite an air.

Tish's plan was very simple. She told us as we cleared up the cave after the day's excitement.

"When I go for the evening milk," she said, "I shall mention that we have a young man with us, a stranger, who has hurt his ankle and cannot walk. And I'll ask for arnica. That's all."

"That's all!" Aggie and I exclaimed together.

"Certainly that's all. Sometime tonight they'll rush the cave."

"You're a fool!" said Aggie shortly.

"Why?" demanded Tish. "We won't be in it. We'll be outside. The moment they are in we'll start to shoot. Not one of them will dare to stick his nose out."

When we told this to Charlie Sands he slid entirely off his chair and sat on the floor. "Not really!" he kept saying over and over. "You dreamed it! You must have! A thing like that!" I hastened to explain. "Tish planned it," I said. I remember him, looking at Tish — who was crocheting as she told the story — and moistening his lips. He was quite green in color.

VI

Clipping from the *Morning News* of May the seventh:

SHERIFF AMBUSHED
Remarkable Experience of Muldoon and Party in Thunder Cloud Glen

An extraordinary state of affairs was discovered by the relief party of constables, city and county detectives and state constabulary sent to the relief of Sheriff Muldoon and his posse, who have been on the track of the C. & L. train bandits since last Monday.

The relief party was sent out in response to a telephone message from a farmhouse in Thunder Cloud Glen, and transmitted from the farmer's line to a long-distance wire. This message was to the effect that the sheriff and his posse, shut in a cave, were being held prisoners by the outlaws, being shot at steadily, and that so far every attempt at escape had been thwarted by the terrific fire of the bandits.

A relief party in automobiles was rushed at once to the scene.

Thunder Cloud Glen is a narrow valley between the Camel's Back and Thunder Cloud Mountain. A mile or so from the entrance to the glen the road, always bad and now almost washed away by the recent heavy rains, became impassable. The party abandoned the machines and in skirmish order proceeded up the glen.

Within an hour's time firing was heard, and the rescuers doubled their pace. Passing a bend in the valley, the scene of the outrage lay spread before them: On the left the low mouth of a cave, and across the valley, on a slope of the Camel's Back, a faint cloud of smoke, showing where the outlaws had their lair. As the rescuers came in sight the firing ceased and an ominous stillness hung over the valley.

The relief expedition had been seen by the imprisoned party also. Muldoon's well-known soft felt hat, tied to the end of a pole, was thrust from the cave mouth and waved vigorously up and down, showing that some of the imprisoned party still lived. One solitary shot was aimed at the hat, followed by profound quiet.

Using every precaution, Deputy Sheriff Mulcahy deployed his men with the intention of closing in on the outlaws from, all sides at the same time.

At this time an interesting interruption occurred. From the underbrush at the foot of the Camel's Back emerged three elderly women, their clothing in tatters, and in the wildest excitement. They insisted that the outlaws were in the cave, and hysterical with fright from their terrible experience, declared that they had been holding the bandits in check and demanded the reward for their capture. They were rational enough in other ways and explained that they had been on a walking tour with a donkey. There was, however, no donkey.

Deputy Sheriff Mulcahy, who is noted for his gallantry, sent the three women to a safe place at the rear of the party and detailed a guard to make them, comfortable. It being thought possible that the women were accomplices of the outlaws, precautions were also taken to prevent their escape.

No trace of the outlaws was found. Sheriff Muldoon and his three deputies, now enabled to leave the cave, joined the searchers. Every inch of Thunder Cloud Glen was searched, but without result. Across from the cave mouth, behind a heap of fallen rocks, was found the spot from which the outlaws had been shooting. The ground was trampled and the rock chipped by the return fire from the cave. Here, too, was found a new automatic revolver, a small rifle and another gun of antique pattern. In a crevice of rock was discovered a flowered-silk bag, containing various articles of feminine use, including a packet of powders marked "hay-fever," a small bottle labeled "blackberry cordial," and a dozen or so unexploded cartridges for the revolver.

Convinced now that the three women were accomplices of the outlaws — and this corroborated by Sheriff Muldoon's statement that he had positively seen one of the three women peering over the rock and aiming a rifle at him, and that the same woman, two days before, had fired at him from the valley, knocking his gun out of his hand — Deputy Sheriff Mulcahy promptly arrested the women and had them taken in an automobile to the city.

At the jail, however, it was discovered that an unfortunate error had been made, and the ladies were released. They went at once to their homes. While their names have not been divulged it is reported that they are well known and highly esteemed members of the community, and much sympathy has been expressed for their disagreeable experience.

Up to a late hour last night no trace had been found of the outlaws. It is believed that they have left Thunder

Cloud Glen and have penetrated farther into the mountains.

Charlie Sands came for us at the jail. He asked us no questions, which I thought strange, but he got a carriage and took us all to Tish's. He did not speak a word on the way, except to ask us if we had no hats. On Tish's replying meekly that we had left them in the cave, he said nothing more, but sat looking like a storm until we drew up at the house.

I dare say we did look curious. Our clothes were torn and draggled, and although we had washed at the jail we were still somewhat powder-streaked and grimy.

Charlie Sands led us into Tish's parlor and shut the door. Then he turned and surveyed the three of us.

"Sit down," he said grimly.

We sat. He stood looking down at each of us in turn.

"I'll hear the story in a minute," he said, still cold and disagreeable. "But first of all, Aunt Tish, I want to ask you if you realize that this last escapade of yours is a disgrace to the family?"

"Nothing of the sort," Tish asserted with something of her old spirit. "It was all for Aggie's missionary dime. I —"

"A moment," he said, holding up his hand. "I'm going to ask a question. I'll listen after that. *Did you or did you not hold up the C. & L. express car?*"

We were too astounded to speak.

"Because if you did," he said, "missionary dime or no missionary dime, I shall turn you over to the authorities! I have gone through a lot with you, Aunt Tish, in the past year."

Aggie and I expected to see Tish rise in majesty and point him out of the room. But to our amazement she broke down and cried.

"No," she said feebly, "we didn't rob the car. But oh, Charlie, Charlie! We nursed that wretch Muldoon, and fed him and sent him off on Modestine in Aggie's gray alpaca, and he got away; and if you say to go to jail I'll go."

"Muldoon!"

"The wretch who said he was Muldoon. The — the train robber."

Well, it took hours to tell the story, and when we had all finished and Aggie had gone to bed in Tish's spare room with hysteria, and Tish had gone to bed with tea and toast, Charlie Sands was still walking up and down the parlor, stopping now and then to mutter: "Well, I'll be — " and then going on with his pacing.

Hannah brought me a cup of junket at eight o'clock, for none of us had eaten dinner. I was sitting there with the cup in my lap when the doorbell rang. Charlie Sands answered it. It was a letter addressed to all three of us.

We called Tish and Aggie and they crept in, very subdued and pallid. Charlie Sands opened the letter and read it:

Dear and Charming Ladies: I am abject. What can I say to you, who have just come through such an experience on my account? How can I apologize or explain? Especially as I am confused myself as to what really happened. Did Muldoon actually attack the cave? Were you in it when he arrived? Or is it possible that, with my foolish fabrication in your mind, you attempted — But that is absurd, of course.

Whatever occurred and however it occurred, I am on my knees to you all. Even a real bandit would have been touched by your kindness. And I am not a real bandit any more than I am a real sheriff.

I am, an ordinary citizen, usually a law-abiding citizen. But as a result of a foolish wager at my club, brought about by the ease with which numerous trains have been robbed recently, I undertook to hold up a C. & L. train with an empty revolver, and to evade capture for a certain length of time. The first part was successful. The train messenger, on seeing my gun, handed me, without a word, a fat package. I had not asked for it. It was a gift. I do not even now know what is in it. The newspapers say it is money. It might have been eggs, as far as I know. The second part would have been simple also, had I not hurt my leg.

Things were looking serious for me when you found me. I shall never forget the cave, or the omelets, or the tea, or the fudge. I can never return your hospitalities, but one thing I can do.

The express company offers a reward of a thousand dollars for my little package. Probably they are right and it is not eggs. Whatever it is, it is buried under the tree where we tied our noble steed, Modestine. Please return the package and claim the reward. If you have scruples against taking it remember that the express company is rich and the Fiji Islanders needy. Turn it in as the increased increment on Miss Aggie's missionary dime.

(Signed)
The Outlaw of Thunder Cloud.

We found the package, or Charlie Sands found it for us, and

the express company paid us the reward. We gave it to Aggie, and with the exception of fifty dollars she turned it all in at the church, where it created almost a riot. With the fifty dollars we purchased, through Charlie Sands, a revolver with a silver inlaid handle, and sent it to the real Sheriff Muldoon. It eased our consciences somewhat.

That was all last spring. It is summer now. Tish is talking again of flowering hedgerows and country lanes, but Aggie and I do not care for the country, and the mere sight of a donkey gives me a chill.

Yesterday evening, on our way to prayer meeting, we heard a great noise of horns coming and stopped to see a four-in-hand go by. A young gentleman was driving, with a pretty girl beside him. As we lined up at the curb he turned smiling from the girl and he caught our eyes.

He started, and then, bowing low, he saluted us from the box.

It was "Muldoon."

TISH DOES HER BIT

From the very beginning of the war Tish was determined to go to France. But she is a truthful woman, and her age kept her from being accepted. She refused, however, to believe that this was the reason, and blamed her rejection on Aggie and myself.

"Age fiddlesticks!" she said, knitting violently. "The plain truth is — and you might as well acknowledge it, Lizzie — that they would take me by myself quick enough, just to get the ambulance I've offered, if for no other reason. But they don't want three middle-aged women, and I don't know that I blame them."

That was during September, I think, and Tish had just received her third rejection. They were willing enough to take the ambulance, but they would not let Tish drive it. I am quite sure it was September, for I remember that Aggie was having hay fever at the time, and she fell to sneezing violently.

Tish put down her knitting and stared at Aggie fixedly until the paroxysm was over.

"Exactly," she observed, coldly. "Imagine me creeping out onto a battlefield to gather up the wounded, and Aggie crawling behind, going off like an alarm clock every time she met a clump of golden rod, or whatever they have in France to produce hay fever."

"I could stay in the ambulance, Tish," Aggie protested.

"I understand," Tish went on, in an inflexible tone, "that those German snipers have got so that they shoot by ear. One sneeze would probably be fatal. Not only that," she went on, turning to me, "but you know perfectly well, Lizzie, that a woman of your weight would be always stepping on brush and sounding like a night attack."

"Not at all," I replied, slightly ruffled. "And for a very good reason. I should not be there. As to my weight, Tish, my mother was always considered merely a fine figure of a woman, and I am just her size. It is only since this rage for skinny women —"

But Tish was not listening. She drew a deep sigh, and picked up her knitting again.

"We'd better not discuss it," she said. But in these days of efficiency it seems a mistake that a woman who can drive an ambulance and can't turn the heel of a stocking properly to save her life, should be knitting socks that any soldier with sense would use to clean his gun with, or to tie around a sore throat, but never to wear.

It was, I think, along in November that Charlie Sands, Tish's nephew, came to see me. He had telephoned, and asked me to have Aggie there. So I called her up, and told her to buy some cigarettes on the way. I remember that she was very irritated when she arrived, although the very soul of gentleness usually.

She came in and slammed a small package onto my table.

"There!" she said. "And don't ever ask me to do such a thing again. The man in the shop winked at me when I said they were not for myself."

However, Aggie is never angry for any length of time, and a moment later she was remarking that Mr. Wiggins had always been a smoker, and that one of his workmen had blamed his fatal accident on the roof to smoke from his pipe getting into his eyes.

Shortly after that I was surprised to find her in tears.

"I was just thinking, Lizzie," she said. "What if Mr. Wiggins had lived, and we had had a son, and he had decided to go and fight!"

She then broke down and sobbed violently, and it was some time before I could calm her. Even then it was not the fact that she had no son which calmed her.

"Of course I'm silly, Lizzie," she said. "I'll stop now. Because of course they don't *all* get killed, or even wounded. He'd probably come out all right, and every one says the training is fine for them."

Charlie Sands came in shortly after, and having kissed us both and tried on a night shirt I was making for the Red Cross, and having found the cookie jar in the pantry and brought it into my sitting room, sat down and came to business.

"Now," he said. "What's she up to?"

He always referred to Tish as "she," to Aggie and myself.

"She has given up going to France," I replied.

"Perhaps! What does Hannah report?"

I am sorry to say that, fearing Tish's impulsive nature, we had felt obliged to have Hannah watch her carefully. Tish has a way of breaking out in unexpected places, like a boil, as Charlie Sands once observed, and by knowing her plans in advance we have sometimes prevented her acting in a rash manner. Sometimes, not always.

"Hannah says everything is quiet," Aggie said. "Dear Tish has apparently given up all thought of going abroad. At least, Hannah says she no longer practises first aid on her. Not since the time Tish gave her an alcohol bath and she caught cold. Hannah says she made her lie uncovered, with the window open, so the alcohol would evaporate. But she gave notice the next day, which was ungrateful of her, for Tish sat up all night feeding her things out of her First Aid case, and if she *did* give her a bit of iodine by mistake —"

"She is no longer interested in First Aid," I broke in. Aggie has a way of going on and on, and it was not necessary to mention the matter of the iodine. "I know that, because I blistered my hand over there the other day, and she merely told me to stick it in the baking soda jar."

"That's curious," said Charlie Sands.

"Because — Great Scott, what's wrong with these cigarettes?"

"They are violet-scented," Aggie explained. "The smell sticks so, and Lizzie is fond of violet."

However, he did not seem to care for them, and appeared positively ashamed. He opened a window, although it was cold outside, and shook himself in front of it like a dog. But all he said was:

"I am a meek person, Aunt Lizzie, and I like to humor whims when I can. But the next time you have a male visitor and offer him a cigarette, for the love of Mike don't tell him those brazen gilt-tipped incense things are mine."

He then ate nine cookies, and explained why he had come.

"I don't like the look of things, beloved and respected spinsters," he said. "I fear my revered aunt is again up to mischief. You haven't heard her say anything more about aeroplanes, have you?"

"No," I replied, for us both.

"Or submarines?"

"She's been taking swimming lessons again," I said, thoughtfully.

"Lizzie!" Aggie cried. "Oh, my poor Tish!"

"I think, however," said Charlie Sands, "that it is not a submarine. There are no submarine flivvers, as I understand it, and a full-size one would run into money. No, I hardly think so. The fact remains, however, that my respected and revered aunt has made away with about seven thousand dollars' worth of bonds that were, until a short time ago, giving semi-annual birth to plump little coupons. The question is, what is she up to?"

But we were unable to help him, and at last he went away. His parting words were:

"Well, there is something in the air, and the only thing to do, I suppose, is to wait until it drops. But when my beloved female relative takes to selling bonds without consulting me, and goes out, as I met her yesterday, with her hat on front side behind, there is something in the wind. I know the symptoms."

Aggie and I kept a close watch on Tish after that, but without result, unless the following incident may be called a result. Although it was rather a cause, after all, for it brought Mr. Culver into our lives.

I think it important to relate it in detail, as in a way it vindicates Tish in her treatment of Mr. Culver, although I do not mean by this statement that there was anything of personal malice in the incident of June fifth of this year. Those of us who know Tish best realize that she needs no defence. Her motives are always of the highest, although perhaps the matter of the police officer was ill-advised. But now that the story is out, and Mr. Ostermaier very uneasy about the wrong name being on the marriage license, I think an explanation will do dear Tish no harm.

I should explain, then, that Tish has retained the old homestead in the country, renting it to a reliable family. And that it has been our annual custom to go there for chestnuts each autumn. On the Sunday following Charlie Sands' visit, therefore, while Aggie and I were having dinner with Tish, I suggested that we make our annual pilgrimage the following day.

"What pilgrimage?" Tish demanded. She was at that time interested in seeing if a table could be set for thirty-five cents a day per person, and the meal was largely beans.

"For chestnuts," I explained.

"I don't think I'll go this year," Tish observed, not looking at either of us. "I'm not a young woman, and climbing a chestnut tree requires youth."

"You could get the farmer's boy," Aggie suggested, hopefully. Aggie is a creature of habit, and clings hard to the past.

"The farmer is not there any more."

We stared at her in amazement, but she was helping herself to boiled dandelion at the time, and made no further explanation.

"Why, Tish!" Aggie exclaimed.

"Aggie," she observed, severely, "if you would only remember that the world is hungry, you would eat your crusts."

"I ate crusts for twenty years," said Aggie, "because I'd been raised to believe they would make my hair curl. But I've come to a time of life when my digestion means more to me than my looks. And since I've had the trouble with my teeth —"

"Teeth or no teeth," said Tish, firmly, "eating crusts is a patriotic duty, Aggie."

She was clearly disinclined to explain about the farm, but on being pressed said she had sent the tenants away because they kept pigs, which was absurd and she knew it.

"Isn't keeping pigs a patriotic duty?" Aggie demanded,

glancing at me across the table. But Tish ignored the question.

"What about the church?" I asked.

Tish has always given the farm money to missions, and is therefore Honorary President of the Missionary Society. She did not reply immediately as she was pouring milk over her cornstarch at the time, but Hannah, her maid, spoke up rather bitterly.

"If we give the heathen what we save on the table, Miss Lizzie," she said, "I guess they'll do pretty well. I'm that fed up with beans that my digestion is all upset. I have to take baking soda after my meals, regular."

Tish looked up at her sharply.

"Entire armies fight on beans," she said

"Yes'm," said Hannah. "I'd fight on 'em too. That's the way they make me feel. And if a German bayonet is any worse than the colic I get —"

"Leave the room," said Tish, in a furious voice, and finished her cornstarch in silence.

But she is a just woman, and although firm in her manner, she is naturally kind. After dinner, seeing that Aggie was genuinely disappointed about the excursion to the farm, she relented and observed that we would go to the farm as usual.

"After all," she said, "chestnuts are nourishing, and might take the place of potatoes in a pinch."

Here we heard a hollow groan from the pantry, but on Tish demanding its reason Hannah said, meekly enough, that she had knocked her crazy bone, and Tish, with her usual magnanimity, did not pursue the subject.

There was a heavy frost that night, and two days later Tish called me up and fixed the following day for the visit to the farm. On looking back, I am inclined to think that her usual enthusiasm was absent, but we suspected nothing. She said that Hannah would put up the luncheon, and that she had looked up the food value of chestnuts and that it was enormous. She particularly requested that Aggie should not bake a cake for the picnic, as has been her custom.

"Cakes," she said, "are a reckless extravagance. In butter, eggs and flour a single chocolate layer cake could support three men at the front for two days, Lizzie," she said.

I repeated this to Aggie, and she was rather resentful. Aggie, I regret to say, has rather a weakness for good food.

"Humph!" she said, bitterly. "Very well, Lizzie. But if she expects me to go out like Balaam's ass and eat dandelions, I'd rather starve."

Neither Aggie nor I is inclined to be suspicious, and although we noticed Tish's rather abstracted expression that morning, we laid it to the fact that Charlie Sands had been talking about going to the American Ambulance in France, which Tish opposed violently, although she was more than anxious to go herself.

Aggie put in her knitting bag the bottle of blackberry cordial without which we rarely travel, as we find it excellent in case of chilling, or indigestion, and even to rub on hornet stings. I was placing the suitcase, in which it is our custom to carry the chestnuts, in the back of the car, when I spied a very small parcel. Aggie saw it too.

"If that's the lunch, Tish," she said, "I don't know that I care to go."

"You can eat chestnuts," said Tish, shortly. "But don't go on my account. It looks like rain anyhow, and the last time I went to the farm in the mud I skidded down a hill backwards and was only stopped by running into a cow that thought I was going the other way."

"Nonsense, Tish," I said. "It hasn't an idea of raining. And if the lunch isn't sufficient, there are generally some hens from the Knowles place that lay in your barn, aren't there?"

"Certainly not," she said stiffly, although it wasn't three months since she had threatened to charge the Knowleses rent for their chickens.

Well, I was puzzled. It is not like Tish to be irritable without reason, although she has undoubtedly a temper. She was most unpleasant on the way out, remarking that if the Ostermaicrs's maid continued to pare away half the potatoes, as any fool could see around their garbage can, she thought the church should reduce his salary. She also stated flatly that she considered that the nation would be better off if some one would uncork a gas bomb in the Capitol at Washington, in spite of the fact that my second cousin, once removed, the Honorable J. C. Willoughby, represents his country in its legislative halls.

It is always a bad sign when Tish talks politics, especially since the income tax.

Although it had no significance for us at the time, she did not put her car in the barn as she usually does, but left it in the road. The house was closed, and there was no cool and refreshing buttermilk with which to wash down our frugal repast, which we ate on the porch, as Tish did not offer to unlock the house. Frugal repast it was indeed, consisting of lettuce sandwiches made without butter, as Tish considered that both butter and lettuce was an extravagance. There were, of course, also beans.

Now as it happens, Aggie is not strong and requires palatable as well as substantial food to enable her to get about, especially to climb trees. We missed her during the meal, and I saw that she was going toward the barn. Tish saw it also, and called to her sharply.

"I am going to get an egg," Aggie replied, with gentle obstinacy. "I am starving, Tish, and I am certain I heard a hen cackle. Probably one of the Knowles's chickens —"

"If it is a Knowles's chicken," Tish said, virtuously, "its egg is a Knowles's egg, and we have no right to it."

I am sorry to relate that here Aggie said: "Oh, rats!" but as she apologized immediately, and let the egg drop, figuratively, of course, peace again hovered over our little party. Only momentarily, however, for, a short time after, a hen undoubtedly cackled, and Aggie got up with an air of determination.

"Tish," she said, "that may be a Knowles's hen or it may be one belonging to this farm. I don't know, and I don't give a — I don't care. I'm going to get it."

"The barn's locked," said Tish.

"I could get in through a window."

I shall never forget Tish's look of scorn as she rose with dignity, and stalked toward the barn.

"I shall go myself, Aggie," she said, as she passed her. "You would probably fall in the rain barrel under the window. You're no climber. And you might as well eat those crusts you've hidden under the porch, if you're as hungry as you make out you are."

"Lizzie," Aggie hissed, when Tish was out of hearing, "*what is in that barn?*"

"It may be anything from a German spy to an aeroplane," I said. "But it's not your business or mine."

"You needn't be so dratted virtuous," Aggie observed, scooping a hole in the petunia bed and burying the crusts in it. "Whatever's on her mind is in that barn."

"Naturally," I observed. "While Tish is in it!"

Tish returned in a short time with one egg, which she placed on the porch floor without a word. But as she made no effort to give Aggie the house key, and as Aggie has never learned to swallow a raw egg, although I have heard that they taste rather like oysters, and slip down in much the same way, Aggie was obliged to continue hungry.

It is only just to record that Tish grew more companionable after luncheon, and got into a large chestnut tree near the house by climbing on top of the hen house. We had always before had the farmer's boy to do the climbing into the upper branches, and I confess to a certain nervousness, especially as Tish, when far above the ground, decided to take off her dress skirt, which was her second best tailor-made, and climb around in her petticoats.

She had to have both hands free to unhook the band, and she very nearly overbalanced while stepping out of it.

"Drat a woman's clothes, anyhow," she said. "If we had any sense we'd wear trousers."

"I understand," I said, "that even trousers are not easy to get out of, Tish."

"Don't be a fool, Lizzie," she said tartly. "If I had trousers on I wouldn't have to take them off. Catch it!"

However, the skirt did not fall clear, but caught on a branch far out, and hung there. Tish broke off a small limb and poked at it from above, and I found a paling from a fence and threw it up to dislodge it. But it stuck tight, and the paling came down and struck Aggie on the head. Had we only known it, this fortunate accident probably saved Aggie's life, for she sat down suddenly on the ground, and said faintly that her skull was fractured.

I was bending over Aggie when I heard a sharp crack from above. I looked up, and Tish was lying full length on a limb, her arm out to reach for the skirt and a most terrible expression on her face. There was another crack, and our poor Tish came hurtling through the air, landing half in Aggie's lap and half in the suitcase.

I was quite unable to speak, and owing, as I learned later, to Tish's head catching her near the waist line, Aggie had no breath even to scream.

There was a dreadful silence. Then Tish said, without moving:

"All my property is to go to Charlie Sands."

"Tish!" I cried, in an agony, and Aggie, who still could not speak, burst into tears.

However, a moment later, Tish drew up first one limb and then the other, and observed that her back was broken. She then mentioned that Aggie was to have her cameo set and the dining room sideboard, and that I was to have the automobile, but the next instant she felt a worm on her neck and sat up, looking rather dishevelled, but far from death.

"Where are you hurt, Tish?" I asked, trembling.

"Everywhere," she replied. "Everywhere, Lizzie. Every bone in my body is broken."

But after a time the aching localized itself in her right arm, which began to swell. We led her down to the creek and got her to hold it in the cold water and Aggie, being still nervous and unsteady, slipped on a mossy stone and sat down in about a foot of water. It was then that our dear Tish became like herself again, for Aggie was shocked into saying, "Oh, damn!" and Tish gave her a severe lecture on profanity.

Tish was quite sure her arm was broken, as well as all the ribs on one side. But she is a brave woman and made little fuss, although she kept poking a finger into her flesh here and there.

"Because," she said, "the First Aid book says that if a lung is punctured the air gets into the tissues, and they crackle on pressure."

It was soon after this that I saw Aggie, who had made no complaint about Tish falling on her, furtively testing her own tissues to see if they crackled.

Leaving my injured there by the creek, I went back to the tree and secured my paling again. By covering it with straw from the barn I was quite sure I could make a comfortable splint for Tish's arm. However, I had but just reached the barn and was preparing to crawl through a window by standing on a rain barrel when I saw Tish limping after me.

"Well?" she said. "What idiotic idea is in your head, Lizzie? Because if it is more eggs —"

"I am going to get some straw and make a splint."

"Nonsense. What for?"

"What do you suppose I intend it for?" I demanded, tartly. "To trim a hat?"

"I won't have a splint."

"Very well," I retorted. "Then I shall get some straw and start a fire to dry Aggie out."

"You'll stick in that window," Tish said, in what, in a smaller woman, would have been a vicious tone.

"Look here, Tish," I said, balancing on the edge of the rain barrel, "is there something in this barn you do not wish me to see?"

She looked at me steadily.

"Yes," she said. "There is, Lizzie. And I'll ask you to promise on your honor not to mention it."

That promise I am glad to say I have kept until now, when the need of secrecy is past, Tish herself having divulged the truth. But at the time I was greatly agitated, and indeed almost fell into the rain barrel.

"Or try to find out what it is," Tish went on, sternly.

I promised, of course, and Tish relaxed somewhat, although I caught her eye on me once or twice, as though she was daring me to so much as guess at the secret.

"Of course, Lizzie," she said, as we approached Aggie, "it is nothing I am ashamed of."

"Of course not," I replied hastily. I took my courage in my hands and faced her. "Tish, have you an aeroplane hidden in that barn?"

"No," she replied promptly. She might have enlarged on her denial, but Aggie took a violent sneezing spell just then, pressing herself between paroxysms to see if she crackled, and we decided to go home at once.

Here a new difficulty presented itself. Tish could not drive the car! I shall never forget my anguish when she turned to me and said:

"You will have to drive us home, Lizzie."

"Never!" I cried.

"It's perfectly easy," she went on. "If children can run them, and the idiots they have in garages and on taxicabs —"

"Never," I said firmly. "It may be easy, but it took you six months, Tish Carberry, and three broken springs and any number of dead chickens and animals, besides the time you went through a bridge, and the night you drove off the end of a dock. It may be easy, but if it is, I'd rather do something hard."

"I shall sit beside you, Lizzie," she said, in a patient voice. "I daresay you know which is your right foot and which is your left. If not, I can tell you. I shall say 'left' when I want you to push out the clutch, and 'right' for the brake. As for gears, I can change them for you with my left hand."

"I could do it sitting in a chair," I said, in a despairing voice. "But Tish," I said, in a last effort, "do you remember when you tried to teach me to ride a bicycle? And that the moment I saw something to avoid I made a mad dash for it?"

"This is different," Tish said. "It is a car —"

"And that I rode about a quarter of a mile into Lake Penzance, and would likely have ridden straight across if I hadn't run into a canoe and upset it?"

"You can always *stop* a car," said Tish. "Don't be a coward, Lizzie. All you have to do is to shove hard with your right foot."

Yet, when I did exactly that, she denied she had ever said it. Fond as I am of Tish, I must admit that she has a way of forgetting things she does not wish to remember.

In the end I consented. It was against my better judgment, and I warned Tish. I have no talent for machinery, but indeed a great fear of it, since the time when as a child I was visiting my grand-aunt's farm and almost lost a finger in a feed-cutter. In addition to that, Tish's accident and her secret had both unnerved me. I knew that calamity faced us as I took my place at the wheel.

Tish was still in her petticoat, as we were obliged to leave her dress skirt in the tree, and Aggie was wrapped in the rug to prevent her taking cold.

"When we meet a buggy," Tish said, "we'd better go past it rather fast. I don't ache to be seen in a seersucker petticoat."

"Fast," I said, bitterly. "You'd better pray that we go past it at all."

However, by going very slowly, I got the thing as far as the gate going into the road. Here there was a hill, and we began to move too rapidly.

"Slower," said Tish. "You've got to make a turn here."

"How?" I cried, frantically.

"Brake!" she yelled.

"Which foot?"

"Right foot. *Right foot!*"

However, it seems that my right foot was on the gas throttle at the time, which she had forgotten. I jammed my foot down hard, and the car seemed to lift out of the air. We went across the ditch, through a stake and rider fence, through a creek and up the other side of the bank, and brought up against a haystack with a terrific jolt.

Tish sat back and straightened her hat with a jerk.

"We'd better go back and do it again, Lizzie," she said, "because you missed one or two things."

"I did what you told me," I replied, sullenly.

"Did you?" said Tish. "I don't remember telling you to leap the creek. Of course, cross-country motoring has its advantages. Only one really should have solid tires, because barbed wire fences might be awkward."

She then sat back and rested.

"Well?" I said.

"Well?" said Tish.

"What am I to do now?"

"Oh!" she said. "I thought you preferred doing it your own way. I don't object, if you don't. You are quite right. Roads do become monotonous. Only I doubt, Lizzie, if you can get over this stack. You'd better go around it."

"Very well," I said. "My own way is to walk home, Tish Carberry. And if you think I am going to steer a runaway automobile you can think again."

Aggie had said nothing, but I now turned and saw her, pale and shaken, taking a sip of the blackberry cordial we always carry with us for emergencies. I suggested that she drive the thing home, but she only shook her head and muttered something about almost falling out of the back end of the car when we leaped up out of the creek. She had, she asserted, been clear up on the folded-back top, and had stayed there until the jolt against the haystack had thrown her forward into the seat again.

I daresay we would still be there had not a young man with a gun run suddenly around the haystack. He had a frightened look, but when he saw us all alive he relaxed. Unfortunately, however, Aggie still had the bottle of blackberry cordial in the air. His expression altered when he saw her, and he said, in a disgusted voice:

"Well, I be damned!"

Tish had not seen Aggie, and merely observed that she felt like that and even more. She then remarked that I had broken her other arm, and her nose, which had struck the wind shield. But the young man merely gave her a scornful glance, and leaning his gun against the haystack, came over to the car and inspected us all with a most scornful expression.

"I thought so!" he said. "When I saw you leaping that fence and jumping the creek, I knew what was wrong. Only I thought it was a party of men. In my wildest dreams — give me that bottle," he ordered Aggie, holding out his hand.

Now it is Aggie's misfortune to have lost her own teeth some years ago, owing to a country dentist who did not know his business. And when excited she has a way of losing her hold, as one may say, on her upper set. She then speaks in a thick tone, with a lisp.

"Thertainly not!" said Aggie.

To my horror, the young man then stepped on the running board of the car and snatched the bottle out of her hand.

"I must say," he said, glaring at us each in turn, "that it is the most disgraceful thing I have ever seen." His eyes stopped at Tish, and traveled over her. "Where is your clothing?" he demanded, fiercely.

It was then that Tish rose and fixed him with a glittering eye.

"Young man," she said, "where my dress skirt is does not concern you. Nor why we are here as we are. Give Miss Pilkington that bottle of blackberry cordial."

"Blackberry cordial!" jeered the young man.

"As for what you evidently surmise, you are a young idiot. I am the President of the local branch of the W. C. T. U."

"Of course you are," said the young man. "I'm Carrie Nation myself. Now watch."

He then selected a large stone and smashed the bottle on it.

"Now," he observed, "come over with the rest of it, and be quick." But here he seemed to realize that Tish's face was rather awful, for he stopped bullying and began to coax. "Now see here," he said. "I'm going to help you out of this if I can, because I rather think it is an accident. You've all had something on an empty stomach. Go down to the creek and get some cold water, and then walk about a bit. I'll see what I can do with the car."

Aggie was weeping in the rear seat by that time, and I shall never forget Tish's face. Suddenly she got out of the car and before he realized what was happening, she had his gun in her good hand.

"Now," she said, waving it about recklessly, "I'll teach you to insult sober and God-fearing women whose only fault is that one of them hasn't all the wit she should have and let a car run away with her. Lizzie, get out of that seat."

It was the young man's turn to look strange.

"Be careful!" he cried. "*Be careful!* It's loaded, and the safety catch —"

"Get out, Aggie."

Aggie crawled out, still holding the rug around where she had sat down in the creek.

"Now," Tish said, addressing the stranger, "you back that car out and get it to the road. And close your mouth. Something is likely to fly into it."

"I beg of you!" said the young man. "Of course I'll do what I can, but — please don't wave that gun around."

"Just a moment," said Tish. "That blackberry cordial was worth about a dollar. Just give a dollar to the lady near you. Aggie, take that dollar. Lizzie, come here and let me rest this gun on your shoulder."

She did, keeping it pointed at the young man, and I could hear her behind me, breathing in short gasps of fury. Nothing could so have enraged Tish as the thing which had happened, and for a time I feared that she would actually do the young man some serious harm.

He sat there looking at us, and he saw, of course, that he had been mistaken. He grew very red, and said:

"I've been an idiot, of course. If you will allow me to apologize —"

"Don't talk," Tish snapped. "You have all you can do without any conversation. Did you ever drive a car before?"

"Not through a haystack," he said in a sulky voice.

But Tish fixed him with a glittering eye, and he started the engine.

Well, he got the car backed and turned around, and we followed him through the stubble as the car bumped and rocked along. But at the edge of the creek he stopped and turned around.

"Look here," he said. "This is suicide. This car will never do it."

"It has just done it," Tish replied, inexorably. "Go on."

"I might get down, but I'll never get up the other side."

"Go on."

"Tish!" Aggie cried, anguished. "He may be killed, and you'll be responsible."

Aggie is a sentimental creature, and the young man was very good-looking. Indeed, arriving at the brink, I myself had qualms. But Tish has a will of iron, and was, besides, still rankling with insult. She merely glued her eye again to the sight of the gun on my shoulder, and said:

"*Go on!*"

Well, he got the car down somehow or other, but nothing would make it climb the other side. It would go up a few feet and then slide back. And at last Tish herself saw that it was hopeless, and told him to turn and go down the creek bed.

It was a very rough creek bed, and one of the springs broke almost at once. We followed along the bank, and I think Tish found a sort of grim humor in seeing the young man bouncing up into the air and coming down on the wheel, for I turned once and found her smiling faintly. However, she merely called to him to be careful of the other springs or she would have to ask him to pay for them.

He stopped then, in a pool about two feet deep, and glared up at her.

"Oh, certainly," he said. "I suppose the fact that I have permanently bent in my floating ribs on this infernal wheel doesn't matter."

At last he came to a shelving bank, and got the car out. I think he contemplated making a run for it then and getting away, but Tish observed that she would shoot into the rear tires if he did so. So he went back to the road, slowly, and there stopped the car.

However, Tish was not through with him. She made him

climb the chestnut tree and bring down her dress skirt, and then turn his back while she put it on. By that time, the young man was in a chastened mood, and he apologized handsomely.

"But I think I have made amends, ladies," he said. "I feel that I shall never be the same again. When I started out today I was a blithe young thing, feeling life in every limb, as the poet says. Now what I feel in every limb does not belong in verse. May I have the shotgun, please?"

But Tish had no confidence in him, and we took the gun with us, arranging to leave it at the first signpost, about a mile away. We left him there, and Aggie reported that he stood in the road staring after us as long as we were in sight.

Tish drove the car home after all, steering with one hand and taking the wheel off a buggy on the way. I sat beside her and changed the gears, and she blamed the buggy wheel on me, owing to my going into reverse when I meant to go ahead slowly. The result was that we began to back unexpectedly, and the man only saved his horse by jumping him over a watering trough.

I have gone into this incident with some care, because the present narrative concerns itself with the young man we met, and with the secret in Tish's barn. At the time, of course, it seemed merely one of the unpleasant things one wishes to forget quickly. Tish's arm was only sprained, and although Aggie wore adhesive plaster around her ribs almost all winter, because she was afraid to have it pulled off, there were no permanent ill effects.

The winter passed quietly enough. Aggie and I made Red Cross dressings for Europe, and Tish, tiring of knitting, made pajamas. She had turned against the government, and almost left the church when she learned that Mr. Ostermaier had voted the Democratic ticket. Then in January, without telling any one, she went away for four days, and Sarah Willoughby wrote me later that the Honorable J. C., her husband, said that a woman resembling Tish had demanded from the gallery of the Senate that we declare war against Germany and had been put out by the Sergeant-at-arms.

I do not know that this was Tish. She returned as unannounced as she had gone, and went back to her pajamas, but she was more quiet than usual, and sometimes, when she was sewing, her lips moved as though she was rehearsing a speech. She observed once or twice that she wanted to do her bit, but that she considered digging trenches considerably easier than driving a sewing machine twelve miles a day.

I remember, in this connection, a conversation I had with

Mrs. Ostermaier some time in January. She asked me to wait after the Red Cross meeting, and I saw trouble in her eye.

"Miss Lizzie," she said, "do you think Miss Tish really enjoys sewing?"

"Not particularly," I admitted. "But it is better than knitting, she says, because it is faster. She likes to get results."

"Exactly," Mrs. Ostermaier observed. "I'll just ask you to look at this pajama coat she has turned in."

Well, there was no getting away from it. It was wrong. Dear Tish had sewed one of the sleeves in the neck opening, and had opened the sleeve hole and faced back the opening and put buttons and buttonholes on it.

"Not only that," said Mrs. Ostermaier, "but she has made the trousers of several suits wrong side before and opened them up the back, and men are such creatures of habit. They like things the way they are used to them."

Well, I had to tell Tish, and she flew into a temper and said Mrs. Ostermaier never could cut things out properly, and she would leave the society. Which she did. But she was very unhappy over it, for Tish is patriotic to her finger tips.

All the spring, until war was declared, she was restless and discontented, and she took to long trips in the car, by herself, returning moodier than ever. But with the announcement of war she found work to do. She made enlisting speeches everywhere, and was very successful, because Tish has a magnetic and compelling eye, and she would fix on one man in the crowd and talk at him and to him until all the men around were watching him. Generally, with every one looking he was ashamed not to come forward, and Tish would take him by the arm and lead him in to the recruiting station.

It was on one of these occasions that we saw the young man of the blackberry cordial again.

Tish saw him first, from the tail of the wagon she was standing in. She fixed him with her eye at once, and a man standing near him, said:

"Go on in, boy. You're as good as in the trenches already. She landed me yesterday, but I've got six toes on one foot. Blessed if she didn't try to take me to a hospital to have one cut off."

"Now," said Tish, "does any one wish to ask any questions?"

I saw the blackberry cordial person take a step forward.

"I would like to ask you one," he said. "How do you reconcile blackberry cordial with the W. C. T. U.?"

Tish went white with anger, and would no doubt have flayed

him with words, as our blackberry cordial is made from her own grandmother's recipe, and a higher principled woman never lived. But unluckily the driver of the furniture wagon we were standing in had returned without our noticing it, and drove off at that moment, taking us with him.

It was about this time that Charlie Sands came to see me one day, looking worried.

"Look here," he said, "what's this about my having appendicitis?"

"Well, you ought to know," I replied rather tartly. "Don't ask me if you have a pain."

"But I haven't," he said, looking aggrieved. "I'm all right. I never felt better."

He then said that once, when a small boy, he had been taken with a severe attack of pain, following a picnic when he had taken considerable lemonade and pickles, followed by ice cream.

"I had forgotten it entirely," he went on. "But the other day Aunt Tish recalled the incident, and suggested that I get my appendix out. It wouldn't matter if she had let it go at that. But she's set on it. I may waken up any morning and find it gone."

I could only stare at him, for he is her favorite nephew, and I could not believe that she would forcibly immolate him on a bed of suffering.

"I used to think she was fond of me," he continued. "But she's — well, she's positively grewsome about the thing. She's talked so much about it that I begin to think I *have* got a pain there. I'm not sure I haven't got it now."

Well, I couldn't understand it. I knew what she thought of him. Had she not, when she fell out of the tree, immediately left him all her property? I told him about that, and indeed about the entire incident, except the secret in the barn. He grew very excited toward the end, however, where we met the blackberry-cordial person, and interrupted me.

"I know it from there on," he said. "Only I thought Culver had made it up, especially about the gun being levelled at him, and the machine in the creek bed. He's on my paper; nice boy, too. Do you mean to say — but I might have known, of course."

He then laughed for a considerable time, although I do not consider the incident funny. But when I told him about Mr. Culver's impertinent question at the recruiting station, he sobered.

"You tell her to keep her hands off him," he said. "I need him in my business. And it won't take much to send him off to war, because he's had a disappointment in love and I'm told that he walks out in front of automobiles daily, hoping to be struck down and make the girl sorry."

"I consider her a very sensible young woman," I observed. But he was already back to his appendix.

"You see," he said, "my Aunt Letitia has a positively uncanny influence over me, and if I have it out I can't enlist. No scars taken."

I put down my knitting.

"Perhaps that is the reason she wants it done," I suggested.

"By George!" he exclaimed.

Well, that *was* the reason. I may as well admit it now. Tish is a fine and spirited woman, and as brave as a lion. But it was soon evident to all of us that she was going to keep Charlie Sands safe if she could. She was continually referring to his having been a sickly baby, and I am quite sure she convinced herself that he had been. She spoke, too, of a small cough he had as indicating weak lungs, and was almost indecently irritated when the chest specialist said that it was from smoking, and that if he had any more lung space the rest of his organs would have had to move out.

One way and another, she kept him from enlisting for quite a time, maintaining that to run a newspaper and keep people properly informed was as patriotic as carrying a gun.

I remember that on one occasion, when he had at last decided to join the navy and was going to Washington, Tish took a very bad attack of indigestion, and nothing quieted her until after train time but to have Charlie Sands beside her, feeding her peppermint and hot water.

Then, at last, the draft bill was passed, and she persuaded him to wait and take his chance.

We were at a Red Cross class, being taught how to take foreign bodies out of the ear, when the news came. Tish was not paying much attention, because she considered that if a soldier got a bullet or shrapnel in his ear, a syringe would not help him much. She had gone out of the room, therefore, and Aggie had just had a bean put in her auditory canal, and was sure it would swell before they got it again, when Tish returned. She said the bill had passed, and that the age limit was thirty-one.

Mrs. Ostermaier, who was using the syringe, let it slip and shot a stream of water into Aggie's right eye.

"Thirty-one!" she said. "Well, I suppose that includes your nephew, Miss Tish."

"Not at all," said Tish. "He will have his thirty-second

birthday on the fifth of June, and he probably won't have to register at all. It's likely to be July before they're ready."

"Oh, the fifth of June!" said Mrs. Ostermaier, and gave Aggie another squirt.

Now Tish and I have talked this over since, and it may only be a coincidence. But Mrs. Ostermaier's cousin is married to a Congressman from the west, and she sends the Ostermaiers all his speeches. Mr. Ostermaier sends on his sermon, too, in exchange, and every now and then Mrs. Ostermaier comes running in to Tish with something delivered in our national legislature which she claims was conceived in our pulpit.

Anyhow, when the draft day was set, *it was the fifth of June*!

Aggie and I went to Tish at once, and found her sitting very quietly with the blinds down, and Hannah snivelling in the kitchen.

"It's that woman," Tish said. "When I think of the things I've done for them, and the way I've headed lists and served church suppers and made potato salad and packed barrels, it makes me sick."

Aggie sat down beside her and put a hand on her knee.

"I know, Tish," she said. "Mr. Wiggins was set on going to the Spanish war. He said that he could not shoot, but that he would be valuable as an observer, from church towers and things, because he was used to being in the air. He would have gone, too, but —"

"If he goes," Tish said, "he will never come back. I know it. I've known it ever since I ran over that black cat the other day."

Well, we had to leave her, as Aggie was buying wool for the Army and Navy League. We went out, very low in our minds. What was our surprise, therefore, on returning late that afternoon, to find Tish cheerfully hoeing in the garden she had planted in the vacant lot next door, while Hannah followed her and gathered up in a basket the pieces of brick, broken bottles and buried bones that Tish unearthed.

"You poor dear!" Aggie said, going toward her. "I know just how you feel. I —"

"Get out!" Tish yelled, in a furious tone. "Look what you're doing! Great heavens, don't you see what you've done? That was a potato plant."

We tried to get out, although I could see nothing but a few weeds, but she yelled at us every moment and at last I gave it up.

"I'd rather stay here, Tish," I said, "if you don't mind. I can keep the dogs away, and along in the autumn, when it's safe to move, you can take me home, or put me in a can, along with the other garden stuff."

Here Tish fired a brick at Hannah's basket, but struck her in the knee cap instead, and down she went on what Tish said was six egg plants. In the resulting conversation I escaped, and went up to Tish's sitting room.

Tish followed us soon after, and jerked the window shades to the top.

"There's nothing like getting close to nature," she said. "I feel like a different woman, after an hour or so of the soil."

She then took Hannah's basket and placed it on the window-sill overlooking the vacant lot, explaining that she used its contents to fling at dogs, cats and birds below.

"It makes a little extra work for Hannah," she commented. "But it's making a new woman of her. It would be good for you, too, Lizzie. There's nothing like bending over to reduce the abdomen."

But Aggie, having come to mourn, proceeded to do it.

"To think," she said, "that if they had only made it a day later, dear Charlie would have been exempt. It's too tragic, Tish."

"I don't know what you are talking about," said Tish in a cold tone. "He does not have to register. He was born at seven in the morning, June fifth."

"In the evening, Tish," said Aggie gently. "I was there, you know, and I remember —"

Tish gave her a terrible look.

"Of course you would know," she observed, icily. "But as I was in the room, and recall distinctly going out and telling old Amanda, the cook, about breakfast —"

"Supper," said Aggie firmly. "You were excited, naturally. But I was in the hall when you came out, and I was expecting my first gentleman caller, which no girl ever forgets, Tish. I remember that Amanda was hooking my dress, which was very tight, because we had waist lines in those days and I wanted —"

"Aggie," Tish thundered, "he was born early in the morning of June fifth. He will be thirty-two years of age early in the morning of Registration day. And if he tries to register I shall be on hand with the facts."

Well, whether she was right or not, she was convinced that she was, and it is useless to argue with her under those circumstances. Luckily she heard a dog in the lot just then, and threw down a broken bottle and some bricks at him, and the woman in the apartment below raised a window and threatened to report her to the Humane Society. But, as usual, Tish was more than her equal.

"Come right up, then," she said. "Because I am a member of the Humane Society and have been for twenty years. I consider throwing bricks at that dog as patriotic a duty as killing a German, any day."

Here, by accident, the basket slid off the window-sill, and Tish closed the window violently.

"It hit her on the head," she said, in what I fear was an exultant tone. "I wouldn't have done it on purpose, but I guess it's no sin to be thankful."

Because the incident I am about to relate concerns not only Registration Day, but also Mr. Culver and the secret in the barn, I have been some time in getting to it. And if, in so doing, I have reflected at any time either on Tish's patriotism or her strict veracity, I am sorry. No one who knows Tish can doubt either.

In spite of Aggie, in spite of Charlie Sands, who protested violently that he distinctly remembered being born in the evening, because he had yelled all the ensuing night and no one had had a wink of sleep — in spite of all this, Tish remained firm in her conviction that 7 A. M. on Registration Day, when the precincts opened, would find him too old to register.

On the surface the days that followed passed uneventfully. Tish sewed and knitted, and once each day stood Aggie and myself on the outskirts of her garden and pointed out things which she said would be green corn, and tomatoes and peppers and so on. But there was a set look about her face, to those of us who knew and loved her. She had moments of abstraction, too, and during one of them weeded out an entire row of spring onions, according to Hannah.

On the third of June I went into the jeweller's to have my watch regulated, and found Tish at the counter. She muttered something about a main spring and went out, leaving me staring after her. I am no idiot, however, although not Tish's mental equal by any means, and I saw that she had been looking at gentlemen's gold watches.

I had a terrible thought that she intended trying to purchase Charlie Sands by a gift. But I might have known her high integrity. She would not stoop to a bribe. And, as a matter of fact, happening to stop at the Ostermaiers' that evening to show Mrs. Ostermaier how to purl, I found that dear Tish, remembering the anniversary of his first sermon to us, had presented Mr. Ostermaier with a handsome watch.

It was on the fourth of June that I had another visit from Charlie Sands. He is usually a most amiable young man, but on that occasion he came in glowering savagely, and on sitting down on Aggie's knitting, which was on steel needles, he flung it across the room, and had to spend quite a little time apologizing.

"The truth is," he said, "I'm so blooming upset that I'm not myself. Let me put these needles back, won't you? Or do they belong in some particular place?"

"They do," Aggie retorted grimly. "And for a young man who will be thirty-two tomorrow morning —"

"Evening," he corrected her, with a sort of groan. "I see she's got you too. Look here," he went on, "I'm in trouble, and I'm blessed if I see my way out. I want to register tomorrow. I may not be drawn, because I'm an unlucky devil and always was. But — I want to do my bit."

"Well," I observed, tartly. "I guess no one can prevent you. Go and do it, and say nothing."

"Not at all," he replied, getting up and striding up and down the room. "Not a bit of it. I grant you it looks simple. Wouldn't any one in his senses think that a young and able-bodied man could go and put his name down as being willing to serve his country? Why, she herself — she's crazy to go. I'd like to bet a hat she'll get there before long, too, and into the front trenches."

"Oh, no!" Aggie wailed suddenly.

"But not I," went on Charlie Sands fiercely. "Not I. How she ever got around that old fool Ostermaier I don't know. But she has. He's appointed her an assistant registrar in his precinct, which is mine. And she'll swear until she's black in the face that I'm over age."

"Can't you have the place opened before seven in the morning?" I suggested.

"I've been to him, but he says the law is seven o'clock. Besides," he added bitterly, "she knows me, and as like as not she'll sleep there, to be on hand to forestall me."

As I look back, I am convinced that a desire to do his bit, as he termed it, was only a part of his anger that evening. The rest was the feeling that Tish's superior acumen had foiled him. He had a truly masculine hatred of being thwarted by a woman, even by a beloved aunt.

"Well," he said at last, picking up his hat. "I'll be off." He went to the door, but turned back and glowered at us both, although I am sure we had done nothing whatever. "But mark my words, and remind her of them the day after tomorrow. This thing's not over yet. She's pretty devilish clever" — (I regret to record this word, but he was greatly excited) — "but she hasn't all the brains in the family."

For a day that was to contain so much, however, the fifth of June started quietly enough. We telephoned Hannah, and she reported that Tish had left the house at five-thirty, although obliged to go only one block to the engine house which was her destination.

So far as I can learn, for Tish is very uncommunicative about the entire matter, the morning passed quietly enough. She had taken the precaution of having her folding card table and two pillows sent to the engine house, and when Aggie and I arrived at midday she was seated comfortably, with her hat hung on a lamp of the fire truck. When we arrived she was asking the sexton of the Methodist Church, whom she has known for thirty years, if he had lost a leg or an arm.

Aggie had brought a basket with some luncheon for her, and she placed it on the truck. But there was an alarm of fire soon after, and the thing went out in a rush with the lunch and also with Tish's hat.

Tish was furiously angry. Indeed, I have since thought that much of what followed was due to the loss of the luncheon, which the firemen declared they had not seen, although Aggie was positive she saw one of them eating one of the doughnuts that afternoon behind a newspaper.

But, worst of all, Tish's hat was missing. It reappeared later, however, but was brought in by the engine house dog, after having been run over by the Chief's machine, two engines and a ladder truck.

As I say, that was part of her irritation, but what really upset her was the number of married men. More than once, as she grew excited, I heard her say:

"Married? How many wives?"

When of course she meant how many children.

She had registered twenty-four married men and two single ones by one o'clock, and she was looking very discouraged. But at one o'clock the clerk from the shoe store at the corner came in, and said he had dependent on him a wife, four children, a mother-in-law, a sister-in-law and his sister-in-law's husband.

"Of course," Tish said bitterly, "you claim exemption."

"Me?" he said. "Me, Miss Carberry? My God, no."

Well, about two o'clock Charlie Sands came in. Tish saw him the moment he entered the door, and stopped work to watch him. But he made no attempt to register. He said he was doing a column of slackers for the next morning's paper.

"There's aren't many," he said, "but of course there are some. The license court is the place to nail them."

"Do you mean to tell me," Tish demanded, "that there are traitors in this country who are getting married *today?*"

"There are," said Charlie Sands, sitting down on the fire truck. "Even so, beloved aunt. They are getting married so they can claim exemption because of a dependent wife. And I'll bet the orphan asylums are full of fellows trying to get ready-made families."

Tish is a composed and self-restrained woman, but she spoke so distinctly of how she felt about such conduct that Charlie Murray, our grocer's assistant, who has four children, did not so much as mention them when she made out his card.

"Of course," Charlie Sands observed, "I don't want to dictate to you, because you're doing all that can be expected of you now. But if some one would go to the license court and tell those fellows a bit of wholesome truth, it might be valuable."

"You do it, Lizzie," Tish said.

"I? I never made a speech in my life, Tish Carberry, and you know it."

"And I never before tried to get the truth from an idiot who says he is twenty-eight and has a daughter of eighteen! See here," Tish said to a man in front of her, waving her pen and throwing a circle of ink about. "I'll have you know that I represent the government today, and if you think you are being funny, you are not."

Well, it turned out that he had married a widow with a child, but had a cork leg anyhow, so it made no difference. But Tish's mind was not on her work. However, she was undecided until Charlie Sands said:

"By the way, I saw your friend Culver among the Cupid-chasers today. And this is his district. You'd better round him up."

"Culver!" Tish said. "Do you mean that — Lizzie, where's my hat?"

Well, we had to recover it again from the engine house dog, whom we found burying it in the back yard. Tish's mind, however, was far away, and she merely brushed it absently with her hand and stuck it on her head. Then she turned to Charlie Sands.

"I'm going to the license court," she said, between clenched teeth. "And I am going to show that young fool that he is not going to hide behind any petticoats today."

"It's his privilege to get married if he wants to."

"When I finish with him," said Tish, grimly, "he won't want to."

All the way to the court house Tish's lips were moving, and I knew she was rehearsing what she meant to say. I think that even then her shrewd and active mind had some foreboding of what was to come, for she called back unexpectedly to Aggie:

"Look in the right-hand pocket and see if there is a box of tacks there."

"Tacks?" said Aggie. "Why, what in the world —"

"I had tacks to nail up flags this morning. Well?"

"They are here, Tish, but no hammer."

"I shan't need a hammer," Tish replied, cryptically.

I am afraid I had expected Tish to lead the way into the license court and break out into patriotic fury. But how little, after all, I knew her! Already in that wonderful brain of hers was seething the plot which was so to alter certain lives, and was to leave an officer of the law — but that comes later on.

Mr. Culver was at the desk. Just as we arrived, a clerk handed him a paper, and he walked across the room to an ice-water cooler and took a drink.

"The slacker!" said Tish, from clenched teeth. "The coward! The poltroon! The —"

At that moment Mr. Culver, with a paper cup in his hand, saw us and stared at us fixedly. The next moment he had whipped off his hat, and was coming toward us.

"Well!" he said, as he came up to us, "so it really did happen!"

Tish took a deep breath, to begin on him, but he went on blithely:

"You see, when I got back home that day, I felt it hadn't really been true. I had *not* gone rabbit-shooting, and found three ladies half-buried in a haystack. And of course I had not driven an automobile along a creek bed and through the old swimming hole, with my own gun levelled at my back."

Tish took another breath and opened her mouth.

"Then, the other day," he went on, smiling cheerfully, "I thought I had had a return of the hallucination, because I fancied I saw you all on a wagon. But the next moment the wagon was driving on, and you were nowhere in sight."

"That was because," said Aggie, "when the wagon started we all sat down unexpectedly, and —"

"Aggie!" Tish said, in a savage tone. "Now, young man, I want to say something to you, and I'd thank you —"

"Oh, I say!" he broke in, looking suddenly depressed, "I can see you are still down on me. But don't scold me. Please don't. Because I am a sensitive person, and you will ruin what was going to be a perfect day. I know I was wrong. I apologize. I eat my words. And now I'll leave you, because if you should vanish into thin air again I should have to go and lock myself up."

Well, with all his gaiety he did not look particularly gay, and he was rather hollow in the cheeks. I came to the conclusion that he was going to marry another young woman, partly to keep out of going to war, but partly to spite the first. I must say I felt rather sorry for him, especially when I saw the way he looked at her. Oh, yes, I picked her out at once, because she never took her eyes off him.

I didn't think she was fooled much, either, because she looked as if she needed to go off into a corner and have a good cry. Well, she got her wish later, if that was what she wanted.

But Tish is a woman of one idea. While he chattered with one eye on the girl, Tish was eyeing him coldly. At last she caught him by the arm.

"I have something to say to you, young man," she commenced. "I want to ask you what you think of any one who —"

"I beg your pardon," he interrupted, and freed his arm. "Awfully sorry. I think a young lady over there wishes to speak to me."

He left us briskly enough, but he slowed up before he got across the room. He stopped once and half turned, too, with the unhappiest face I've ever seen on a human being. Aggie was feeling in her knitting bag for the glasses.

"Is she pretty?" she asked.

"Too pretty to be a second choice," I replied, shortly. "She's a nice little thing, and deserves something better than a warmed-over heart."

Tish had been angry enough before, but when I told her that he had been disappointed in love, and was merely making the girl a tool, her eyes were savage.

"She is pretty," Aggie observed. "Perhaps, after all, he *does* love her. Or if not he may learn to. And he cannot be very unhappy about marrying her. He said, you know, it was a perfect day."

"Go down and get into the car," Tish said, in a choking voice. "I'll fix his perfect day for him. Go down and start the engine."

I took a last glance as Aggie and I left the License Court, and if we had had any doubts they vanished then, because he was speaking to the girl with angry gestures, and she was certainly crying.

"Brute," Tish said, with her eyes on him. "A bully as well as a slacker. Never mind. She won't have to put up with him long. If I have any influence in this community that youth will be drafted and sent to a mud hole in France. Mark my words," she went on, settling her hat with a jerk, "that boy will be registered as a single man before this day's over. Go and start the engine, Lizzie. I daresay you remember that much."

Seeing that she had a plan, and "ours not to reason why, ours but to do and die," as Aggie frequently quotes, we went down to the street again. I was even then vaguely apprehensive, an apprehension not without reason, as it turned out. For, reaching over to start the engine, as Tish had taught me by turning a lever on the dashboard and moving up a throttle on the wheel, what was my horror to see the car moving slowly off, with Aggie in the rear seat and as white as chalk.

Tish, in her patriotic fervor, had stopped the thing in gear.

I ran beside it, but was unable to get onto the running board. I then saw Aggie, generally so timid, crawling over the back of the seat, and called to her to put on the brake. She did so, but not until the car had mounted the sidewalk and struck a policeman in the back.

This would not be worth recording, as there were no immediate results, had it not been for the policeman. It brought us to his attention, and came near to ruining Tish's plan. But of this later on.

I do not, even now, know just what arguments Tish used with Myrtle. Yes, that was her name. We had a great deal of time later on to learn her name, and all about her. The matter is a delicate one, and we have not since discussed the events of that day. But Aggie said later on, when we were sitting in the dark and wondering what to do next, that Tish had probably waited until Mr. Culver went out to look up a minister.

Whatever Tish said or did, the result was that only a short time after Aggie had jammed on the brake, they came out together, and Tish was carrying a suitcase. Myrtle was hanging back, but Tish had her by the arm.

At first she did not see us. When she did, however, she worked her way through the crowd and opened the rear door.

"Get in," she said, in an uncompromising tone.

"But I really think," said Myrtle, "that I should —"

"Get in," Tish said again, firmly. "We can talk it over later."

"But are you sure he sent for me?" she demanded, looking ready to cry again. "I think it must be a mistake. He said to wait, and he would come back as soon as —"

It was the crowd that really settled the matter, for some one yelled that the girl had been eloping and that her mother had caught her in the License Court. Most of them were men, but they called to Myrtle not to let the old lady bully her. Also one young man said that if her young man didn't come back she could have him and welcome. It frightened Myrtle, and she got into the car and asked Tish to drive away quickly.

"I know it will be in the papers," she said forlornly. "And my people think I am at a house party."

But the next moment I caught her looking at Tish's hat, and her lip quivered.

"I guess I'm nervous," she said, in a choking voice. "I had no idea it was so much trouble to get married."

Tish heard her, although she had her hands full getting the car back to the street. She said nothing until we were in the street again, and moving away slowly.

"Then you might as well settle down and be quiet," she said. "Because you are not going to be married today."

Myrtle may have suspected something before that, perhaps when she first saw Tish's hat, for she looked dazed for a moment, and then stood up in the car and yelled that she was being kidnapped. Tish threw on the gas just then, and she had to sit down, but I looked back just in time to see Mr. Culver and the policeman standing in the center of the street, gesticulating madly.

"Little fool!" Tish muttered, and bent low over the wheel.

Well, they followed us. At the top of the first hill the girl was crying hard, and there were eleven automobiles, Aggie counted, not far behind us. At the end of the next rise there were still ten. It was then that Tish, with her customary presence of mind, told us to scatter the tacks over the road behind us.

The result was that only four were to be seen when we got to the top of Graham's Hill, and they had lost time and were far away. Tish was in a terrible way. Her plan had been merely to take the girl away, because Culver belonged in her precinct and it was her business, as ordered by the government, to gather in all the slackers, matrimonial or otherwise. Then, after Culver had registered as a single man, he could, as Tish tersely observed later, either marry or go and drown himself. It was immaterial to her.

But now we were likely to be arrested for abduction, and the whole thing would get in the papers.

"Tish," Aggie begged, "do stop and put her out in the road. That Culver and the policeman are in the first car. I can see them plainly — and they can pick her up and take her back."

But Tish ignored her, and kept on. She merely asked, once, if we had any scissors with us, and on Aggie finding a pair in her knitting bag, said to get them out and have them ready.

I pause here for a moment to reflect on Tish's resourcefulness. How many times, in the years of our association, has her active brain come to our rescue in trying times? And, once the danger is over, how quickly she becomes again one of us, busy with her charities, her Sunday school class, and her knitting for the poor! Indomitable spirit and Christian soul, her only fault, if any, perhaps a slight lack of humor, that is Letitia Carberry.

"Watch for a barbed wire fence, Lizzie," she said, as we flew along. "And see how near they are."

Well, they were very close, but owing to Tish leaving the macadam at this point, they lost time at a crossroads. At the top of the next hill Aggie said she could not see anything of them. It was then that Myrtle tried to jump out, and would have succeeded had not Tish speeded up the car.

I could hear Aggie trying to soothe her, and telling her that Tish was not insane, but was merely saving her from a terrible fate.

"I have never been married, my dear, owing to an unfortunate circumstance," she said, in her gentle voice. "But to marry without love —"

The girl sat up, startled.

"But how do you know I don't love him?" she demanded.

"I am speaking of the young man," said Aggie. "My dear child, all over this great land of ours today, here and there are wretches who would use a confiding young woman in order —"

"Barbed wire!" said Tish exultantly, and stopped the car with a jerk. In an instant she was out in the road, cutting lengths of barbed wire from a fence with the scissors and placing them across the road behind us. Her expression was set and tense. When she had placed some six pieces of wire in position, she returned to the car.

"We can thank the war for that," she observed, coolly. "As long as the barbed wire fences hold out they'll never get us."

The first car was in sight by that time, and we could see that Mr. Culver and the policeman were in it. They shouted with joy when they saw us, but Tish merely smiled, and let in the clutch. Soon after we heard a series of small explosions, and Tish observed that the enemy attack was checked against our barbed wire, and that she reckoned we could hold the position indefinitely.

Aggie looked back and reported that they were both out of the car, and that the policeman was standing on one foot and hopping up and down.

It had been Tish's intention, as I learned later, merely to take the young woman for a country ride, and there to strive to instill into her the weakness and folly of being married by Mr. Culver as an exemption plea. But as we had been making forty-five miles an hour by the speedometer, there had been little opportunity.

However, as the last car was now standing on four rims in the barbed wire entanglement behind us, and as Tish's farm was not far ahead, she improved the occasion with a short but highly patriotic speech, flung over her shoulder.

"I don't believe it," said Myrtle, sullenly. "He loves me. We only ran away today instead of some other day later because my father is leading the parade in my town, and mother is presenting a flag at the schoolhouse."

"Very well," said Tish. "If he loves you, well and good. When your young man has registered, I'll see that you get married, if I have to kidnap a preacher to do it. But I'll tell you right now, I don't think you'll be getting anything worth having."

Well, Myrtle grew quieter then, and I heard Aggie saying Miss Tish never made a promise she could not fulfill. She then told about Mr. Wiggins, and had just reached the place where he had slipped on the eve of his wedding and fallen off a roof, when the car stopped dead.

Tish pushed a few things on the dashboard, but it only hiccoughed twice and then stopped breathing.

"No gasoline!" she exclaimed, in a rage. "We'll have to run for it."

The farmhouse was in sight now, about a half mile ahead. Aggie groaned, but got out and turned to Myrtle. But Myrtle was sitting back in the car with a gleam of triumph in her eyes.

"Certainly *not*," she said calmly.

"Very well," Tish replied. "I don't know but you are just as well where you are. That last car is done for, if I know anything about barbed wire, and they're not likely to chase a machine on foot. They're probably on their way back to town now, and I hope the policeman has to hop all the way. It's only forty miles or so."

She then started up the road, but turned:

"Bring her suitcase, Lizzie," she said. "There's no use leaving it there for tramps to come along and steal it."

She then stalked majestically up the road, and we followed. I am not a complaining woman, but if that girl had left any clothes at home they couldn't have amounted to much. Aggie refused to help with the suitcase, as she had her knitting bag, and as any exertion in summer brings on her hay fever.

It was perhaps five minutes later that I heard a faint call behind me, and turned to see Myrtle coming along behind. She was not crying now, and her mouth was shut tight.

"I suppose," she said angrily, "that it does not matter if tramps get *me*."

"Miss Tish invited you to the farm," I replied.

"Invited!" she snapped. "If this is what she calls an invitation, I'd hate to have her make it a request."

However, she seemed to be really a very nice girl, although misguided, for she took one end of the suitcase. But I learned then how difficult it is for the average mind to grasp the high moral purpose and lofty conception of a woman like Tish.

"I might as well tell you now," she said, "that I don't believe they'll pay any large sum. They're not going to be very keen about me at home, since this elopement business."

"Who'll pay what sum?"

"The ransom," she said, impatiently. "You don't suppose I fell for all that patriotic stuff, do you?"

I could only stare at her in dumb rage.

"At first, of course," she said, "I thought you were white slavers. But I've got it now. The other game is different. Oh, I may come from a small town, but I'm not unsophisticated. You people didn't send my father those black hand letters he's been getting lately, I suppose?"

"Tish!" I called sharply.

But Tish had stopped and was listening intently. Suddenly she said:

"Run!"

There was a sort of pounding noise somewhere behind, and Aggie screeched that it was the Knowleses' bull loose on the road. I thought it quite likely, and as we had once had a very unpleasant time with it, spending the entire night in the Knowleses' pig pen, with the animal putting his horns through the chinks every now and then, I dropped the suitcase and ran. Myrtle ran too, and we reached the farmhouse in safety.

It was then that we realized that the sound was the pursuing car, bumping along slowly on four flat tires. Tish shut and bolted the door, and as the windows were closed with wooden frames, nailed on, we were then in darkness. We could hear the runabout, however, thudding slowly up the drive, and the voices of Mr. Culver and the policeman as they tried the door and the window shutters.

Tish stood just inside the door, and Myrtle was just beside me. Aggie had collapsed on a hall chair. I have, I think, neglected to say that the farmhouse was furnished. Tish's mother used to go out there every summer, and she was a great woman for being comfortable.

At last Mr. Culver came to the front door and spoke through it.

"Hello, inside there!" he called, in a furious voice. As no one replied, he then banged at the door, and from the sound I fancy the policeman was hammering also, with his mace.

"Open, in the name of the law!" bellowed the policeman.

"Stop that racket," Tish replied sternly. "Or I shall fire."

Of course she had no weapon, but they did not know this. We could hear Mr. Culver telling the policeman to keep back, as he knew us, and we had any other set of desperadoes he had ever heard of beaten for recklessness with a gun.

There was a moment's silence, during which I heard Aggie's knitting needles going furiously. She learned to knit by touch once when she had iritis and was obliged to finish a slumber robe in time for Tish's birthday. So the darkness did not trouble her, and I knew she was knitting to compose herself.

Tish then stood inside the door, and delivered through it one of the most inspiring patriotic speeches I have ever heard. She spoke of our long tolerance, while the world waited. Then of the decision, and the call to arms. She said that the sons of the Nation were rising that day in their might.

"But," she finished, "there are some among us who would shirk, would avoid the high and lofty duty. There are some who would profane the name of love, and hide behind it to save their own cowardly skins. To these ignoble ones there is but one course left open. Go. Put your name on the roster of your country as a free man, unmarried and without impediments of any sort. Then return and these doors will fly open before the magic of a blue card."

It was at that time, we learned later, that the policeman, who was but a rough and untutored type, decided that Tish was insane — how often, alas, is genius thus mistaken! — and started off for the Knowles farm to bring help. Mr. Culver made no reply to Tish's speech, and we learned later had gone away in the midst of it. Later on he was reported by Aggie, who looked out from an upper window, to be sitting under the chestnut tree where he had once rescued Tish's black alpaca skirt, sulking and watching.

Tish then went up and spoke to him from the window.

"See here," she said angrily, "do you think that I did not mean what I said through that door?"

He had the audacity to yawn.

"I didn't hear all of it," he said. "But judging from what I know of you, I daresay you meant it. Would you mind tossing me a tin cup or something to drink out of?"

"You are not going back to town to register, then?"

"It's early," he replied, coolly. "If you mean do I intend to walk back, I do not. I shall wait for the Sheriff and the posse."

It was then that Tish saw the policeman crossing a field toward the Knowles farm and she tried to reason with the young man. But he dropped his pretence of indifference, and would not even listen to her.

"I've only one thing to say," he said, fiercely. "You be careful of that young lady. As to whether I register or not, that's my business and has nothing to do with the case. When you open that door and send her out, with four good tires to take the place of the ones you ruined, I'll talk to you, and not before."

He then got up and walked away, and Tish came downstairs and lighted a candle with hands that shook with rage. We had heard the entire conversation, and in the candlelight I could see that Aggie was as white as wax.

Well, the situation was really desperate, but Tish's face forbade questions. Aggie ventured to observe that perhaps it would be better to unlock the door and release the girl, but Tish only gave her a ferocious glance.

"I am doing my duty," she said, firmly. "I have done nothing for which the law can punish me. If a young lady comes willingly into my car for a ride, as you did" — she turned sharply to Myrtle — "and if a young fool chooses to sit in my front yard instead of registering to serve his country, it is not my fault. As a matter of fact, I can probably have him arrested for trespass."

As I have said, the farmhouse is still furnished with Tish's mother's things. She was a Biggs, and all the things the Biggses had not wanted for sixty years were in the house. So at least we had chairs to sit on, and if we had only had water, for we were all thirsty from excitement and dust, we could have been fairly comfortable, although Myrtle complained bitterly of thirst.

"And I want to wash," she said fretfully. "If I could wash I'd change my blouse and look like something."

"For whom?" Tish demanded. "For that slacker outside?"

Suddenly Myrtle laughed. She had been in tears for so long that it surprised us. We all stared at her, but she seemed to get worse and worse.

"She's hysterical, poor child," Aggie said, feeling for her smelling salts. "I don't know that I blame her, Tish. No one knows better than I do what it is to expect to be married, and then find the divine hand of Providence intervening."

But Myrtle suddenly walked over to Aggie and, stooping, kissed her on the top of her right ear.

"You dear thing!" she said. "I still don't get all the idea, but I don't much care if I don't. I haven't had so much excitement since I ran away from boarding school."

She then straightened and looked at Tish. It was clear that her feeling for dear Tish was still vague, but was rather more of respect than of love.

"As for the — the young man outside," she said, "I seem to gather that he hasn't registered, and that I am not to marry him until he has. Very well. I hadn't thought about it before, but that speech of yours — suppose you tell him that I won't marry him until he has a — a magic blue card. I should like to see his face."

But Tish is a woman of delicacy, and she suggested that Myrtle do it herself, from an upper window. I went up with her, and we found Mr. Culver again under the tree. The conversation ran like this:

Myrtle, (looking very pretty indeed but very firm): Look here, I — I've decided not to marry you.

Mr. Culver (rousing suddenly and staring up at her): I beg your pardon!

Myrtle: I know now that I was making a terrible mistake. No matter how much I care for you, I cannot marry a slacker.

Mr. C. (furiously angry and glaring at her): You know better than that!

Myrtle: Not at all. Can you deny that you haven't registered yet?

Mr. C.: What's that got to do with it? I daresay I'm losing my mind. It wouldn't be much wonder if I have. When I think of the way I've suffered lately — look at me!

Myrtle (in a somewhat softened voice): Have you really suffered?

Mr. C.: I? Good Lord, Myrtle — why, I haven't slept for weeks. I —

But here he stopped, with his eyes fixed on the roof overhead.

"Watch out!" he yelled. "Get back. Myrtle, she'll fall on you."

"Not at all," said Tish's calm voice from overhead. There was a rasping sound, and then a long wire fell past the window. "Now," she called triumphantly, "let your policeman telephone for the Sheriff and a posse! That was a party wire, and that farmhouse over there is on it. There isn't another telephone for ten miles."

Well, I looked around for Myrtle, and she was on the guest room bed, face down.

"Oh," she groaned, "I wouldn't have missed it for a trip to Europe. And his face! Miss Lizzie, did you see his face?" She then got up suddenly and put her arms around me. "I'm simply madly happy, Miss Lizzie," she said. "I have to kiss somebody, and since he — may I kiss you?"

Well, of course I allowed her to, but I was surprised. It was not natural, somehow.

Myrtle came down soon after and said that Mr. Culver was bringing some water from the well, and would he be allowed to come in with it? But Tish was firm on this point. She gave her consent, however, to his leaving the pail on the porch and then retiring to the chestnut tree. He did so, whistling to signify that he was at a safe distance, and I then carried it in.

"I say," he called to me when he saw me, "this situation is getting on my nerves. I carried off that policeman, for one thing. He was on duty."

"You needn't stay here."

"I daresay not," he replied rather bitterly. "But what I want to ask is this: Won't it be deucedly unpleasant for you three, when I report that you deliberately put my car out of commission so I could not get back by nine o'clock to register? Of course," he went on, "a box of tacks may have spilled itself on the road, but I never heard of a barbed wire fence trying to crawl across a road and getting run over, like a snake."

I reported this to Tish, and I saw that she was uneasy, although she merely remarked that he still had two legs, and that she had not asked him to follow us. All she had set out to do was to see that he didn't get married before he registered, and she was doing that to the best of her ability. The rest was his affair.

It was six o'clock by that time, and Tish had had nothing to eat since five in the morning, and none of us had had any luncheon. Although a woman who thinks little or nothing of food, I found her, shortly afterwards, in the pantry, looking into jars. There was nothing, however, except some salt, a little baking powder and a package of dried sage. But Aggie, going to an attic window to look for the policeman, discovered about a quart of flour in a barrel up there, and scraping it out, brought it down.

"I might bake some biscuits, Tish," she suggested. "I feel that I'll have to have some nourishment. I'm so weak that my knees shake."

"Myrtle," Tish said abruptly, with that quick decision so characteristic of her, "you might tell that worthless young man of yours to look in the granary. Sometimes the Knowleses' hens come over here, and I daresay they've eaten enough off the place to pay for the eggs."

But Myrtle, after a conference from the window, reported that Mr. Culver had said he would get the eggs, if there were any, on condition that he get his pro rata share of them.

"If there are ten eggs," she said, "he wants two. And if there is an odd number he claims the odd one."

This irritated Tish, but at last she grudgingly consented. In a short time, therefore, Mr. Culver knocked at the kitchen door.

"I am leaving," he said, "eleven eggs, eight of undoubted respectability, two questionable, and one that I should advise opening into a saucer first. Also some corn meal from the granary. And if you will set out a pail and come after me if I am wounded, I shall go after a cow that I see in yon sylvan vale."

His voice was strangely cheerful, but, indeed, the prospect of food had cheered us all, although I could see that Tish was growing more and more anxious, as time went on and no policeman appeared in the Knowleses' machine. However, we worked busily. Myrtle, building a fire and setting the table with the Biggses' dishes, and Aggie making biscuits, without shortening, while Tish stirred the corn meal mush.

"Many a soldier in the trenches," she said, "would be grateful for such a frugal meal. When one reflects that the total cost of mush and milk is but a trifle —"

Here, however, we were interrupted by Mr. Culver outside. He spoke in gasps and we heard the pail clatter to the porch floor.

"I regretfully report — " he said, through the keyhole. "No milk. Wrong sex. Sorry."

Ten of the eggs proving good, we placed two of them on a plate with three biscuits and a bowl of mush, and Tish carried it out, placing it on the floor of the porch, much as she would have set it out for the dog.

"Here," she called. "And when you have finished you might go after that accomplice of yours. He's probably asleep somewhere."

"Dear lady," said Mr. Culver, "I would, but I dare not. A fiery creature, breathing fury from its nostrils, is abroad and —"

But Tish came in and slammed the door.

It was after supper that we missed Tish. She was nowhere in the house, and the kitchen door, which had been bolted, was unlocked. Aggie wrung her hands, but Myrtle was quite calm.

"I shouldn't worry about her," she said. "She's about as well able to take care of herself as any woman I ever saw."

It was now quite dark, and our fears increased. But soon afterwards Tish came in. She went to the stove and pouring out a cup of hot water, drank it in silence. Then she said:

"I've been to the Knowleses'. The dratted idiots are all away, probably to the schoolhouse, registering. The car's gone, and the house is closed."

"And the policeman?" I asked.

"I didn't see him," said Tish. But she did not look at me. She fell to pacing up and down the kitchen, deep in thought.

"What time is it, Lizzie?" she asked.

"Almost eight."

Here Tish gave what in another woman would have been a groan.

"It's raining," she observed, and fell to pacing again. At last she told me to follow her outside, and I went, feeling that she had at last made a decision. Her attitude throughout her period of cogitation had been not unlike that of Napoleon before Waterloo. There were the same bent head and clasped hands, the same melancholy mixed with determination.

Mr. Culver was sitting under his tree, with his coat collar turned up around his neck. Tish stopped and surveyed him with gentle dignity.

"You may enter the house," she said. "The country will gain nothing by your having pneumonia, although personally I am indifferent. And, after thinking over your case, I have come to this decision." She paused, as for oratorical effect. "I shall deliver you to your registration precinct by nine o'clock," she said impressively, "and immediately after that, I shall see that you two are married. I am not young," she went on, "and perhaps I do not think enough of sentiment. But it shall never be said of me that I parted two loving hearts, one of which may, before the snow flies, be still and pulseless in a foreign grave."

She then, still with that new air of melancholy majesty, led me to the barn, leaving him staring.

It was there, by means of a key hanging round her neck, that Letitia Carberry, great hearted woman and patriot that she is, bared her inner heart to me. In the barn was a large and handsome ambulance, with large red crosses on side and top, which she had offered to the government if she might drive it herself. But the government which she was even then so heroically serving had refused her permission, and Tish had buried her disappointment in the bucolic solitude of her farm.

Such, in brief, was Tish's tragic secret.

"I shall take it in to the city tonight, Lizzie," she said heavily. "And tomorrow I shall present it to the Red Cross. Some other hand than mine will steer it through shot and shell, and ultimately into Berlin. It has everything. There's a soup compartment and — well," she finished, "it is doing its work even tonight. Get in."

We found Aggie on the porch, having with her usual delicacy of feeling left the lovers alone inside. When she saw the Ambulance, however, she fell to sneezing violently, crying out between paroxysms that if Tish was going to the war, she was also. But Tish hushed her sternly.

There was a good engine in the Ambulance. Tish said she had ordered a fast one, because it was often necessary to run between shells, as it were. She then shoved on the gas as far as it would go, and we were off. After a time, finding it impossible to sit on the folding seats inside, we all sat on the floor, and I believe Mr. Culver held Myrtle's hand all of the way.

He said little, beyond observing once that he felt a trifle queer about leaving the policeman, who had been on duty when he picked him up at the Court House, and who was now lost some forty-five miles from home, in a strange land.

I am glad, in this public manner, to correct the report that on the evening of June fifth a German Zeppelin made a raid over our country, and that the wounded were hurried to the city in a Red Cross Ambulance, traveling at break-neck speed.

At nine o'clock Mr. Culver was registered at Engine House number eleven, fourteenth ward, third precinct.

At nine-fifteen Mr. Culver and Myrtle were married at the same address by Mr. Ostermaier, standing in front of the fire truck.

But this should be related in detail. So bitter was Charlie Sands, so uneasy about the license, and so on, that I feel in fairness to Tish that I should relate exactly what happened.

At ten o'clock that night everything was over, and we had gathered in Tish's apartment while Hannah broiled a steak, for Tish felt that the occasion permitted a certain extravagance, when Charlie Sands came in. Behind him was a dishevelled young man, with wild eyes and a suitcase. Charlie Sands stood and glared at us.

"Well!" he said. And then: "Where's the young lady?"

"What young lady?" asked Tish, coldly.

The young man stepped forward, with his fists clenched.

"Mine!" he bellowed. "Mine! Don't deny it. I recognize you. I saw you — the lot of you. I saw you drag her into a car and kidnap her. I saw that ass Culver and a policeman chasing you in another car. Oh, I know you, all right. Didn't I pay twenty-two dollars for a taxicab that got three punctures all at once thirty miles from the city? *Now where is she?*"

"Just a moment," said Tish's nephew, holding him back by an arm across his chest. "Just remember that whatever my aunt has done was done with the best intentions."

"D — her intentions! I want Myrtle."

The dreadful truth must have come to Tish at that moment, as it did to the rest of us. I know that she turned pale. But she rose and pointed magnificently to the door.

"Leave my apartment," she said majestically. And to Charlie Sands: "Take that madman away and lock him up. Then, if you have anything to say to me, come back alone."

"Not a step," said the young man. "Where's my marriage license? Where's —"

But Charlie Sands pushed him out into the hallway and closed the door on him. Then, with folded arms he surveyed us.

"That's right!" he said. "Knot! I believe most pirates knit on off days. Now, Aunt Letitia, I want the whole story."

"Story?"

"About the license. He says the girl had the license."

"What license?"

"Don't evade!" he said sternly. "Where were you this afternoon?"

"If you want the truth," said Tish, "although it's none of your business, Charlie Sands, and you can unfold your arms, because the pose has no effect on me, — I was out rounding up a young man who had not registered. I got him and brought him in to my precinct at five minutes to nine."

"And that's the truth?"

"Go and ask Mr. Ostermaier," said Tish, in a bored tone.

"But this boy outside —"

"Look here," Tish said suddenly, "go and ask that noisy young idiot for his blue card. It's my belief he hasn't registered and more than likely he's been making all this fuss so he'll have an excuse if he's found out. How do we know," she went on, gaining force with each word, "that there *is* a Myrtle?"

"By George!" said Charlie Sands, and disappeared.

It was then, for the first time in her valiant life, that I saw our Tish weaken.

"Lizzie!" she groaned, leaning back in her chair. "That Culver was married with another man's name on the license. What's more, I married him to that flibbertygibbet who had just jilted him. What have I done? Oh, what have I done?"

"They both seemed happy, Tish," I tried to soothe her. But she refused all consolation, and merely called Hannah and asked for some blackberry cordial. She drank fully half a tumbler full and she recovered her poise by the time Charlie Sands stuck his head through the door again.

"You're right, most shrewd of aunts," he said. "He's been playing me for a sucker all right. Not a blue card on him! And he belongs out of town, so it's too late."

"It's a jail matter," said Tish, knitting calmly, although we afterwards discovered that she had put a heel on the wristlet she was making. "You'd better get his name, and I'll notify the sheriff of his county in the morning."

Charlie Sands came over to her and stood looking down at her.

"Aunt Tish," he said. "I believe you. I believe you firmly. I shall not even ask about a young man named Culver, who went to get our marriage license list at the Court House this afternoon and has not been seen since. But I want to bring a small matter to your attention. That policeman had not registered."

He then turned and went toward the door.

"But I did, dear Aunt Letitia," he said and was gone.

Tish came to see me the next afternoon, bringing the paper, which contained a glowing account of her gift to the local Red Cross of a fine ambulance. An editorial comment spoke of her public spirit, which for so many years had made her a conspicuous figure in all civic work.

"The city," it finished, "can do with many like our Miss 'Tish' Carberry."

But Tish showed no exultation. She sat in a rocking chair and rocked slowly.

"Read the next editorial, Lizzie," she said, in a low voice.

I have it before me now, cut out rather raggedly, for I confess I was far from calm when I did it.

"A SHAMEFUL INCIDENT.

"Perhaps nothing has so exposed this city to criticism as the conduct of Officer Flinn, as shown in a news item in our columns exclusively. Officer Flinn has been five years on the police force of this city. He has until now borne an excellent record. But he did not register yesterday, and on limping into the Central Station this morning told a story manifestly intended to indicate temporary insanity and thus still further disqualify him for the service of his country. His statement of seeing three elderly women kidnap a young girl from in front of the Court House, his further statement of following the kidnappers far into the country, with a young man he cannot now produce, is sufficiently outrageous.

"But, not satisfied with this, the inventive ex-officer went further and added a night in a pigpen, constantly threatened by a savage bull, and a journey of forty-five miles on foot when, early this morning, the animal retired for a belated sleep!

"Representatives of this paper, investigating this curious situation, found the farmhouse which Officer Flinn described as being the den of the kidnappers and which he stated he had left in a state of siege, the bandits and their victim within and the young man who had accompanied the officer, without. Needless to say, nothing bore out his story. A young married couple, named Culver, who are spending their honeymoon there, knew nothing of the circumstances, although stating that they believed that a neighboring family possessed a belligerent bull.

"It is a regrettable fact that the only scandal which marred a fine and patriotic outburst of national feeling yesterday should have involved the city organization. Is it not time that loyal citizens demand an investigation into —"

"Never mind the rest, Lizzie," Tish said wearily. "I suppose I'll have to get him something to do, but I don't know what, unless I employ him to follow me around and arrest me when I act like a dratted fool."

She sighed, and rocked slowly.

"Another thing, Lizzie," she said. "I don't know but what Aggie was right about Charlie Sands. I've been thinking it over, and I guess it was evening, for I remember seeing a new moon just before he came, and wishing he would be a girl. But I guess I was too late. If I'd known about this war, I'd have wished it sooner. I'm a broken woman, Lizzie," she finished.

She put on her hat wrong side before, but I had not the heart to tell her, and went away.

However, late that evening she called me up, and her voice was not the voice of a broken creature.

"I thought you might like to come over, Lizzie," she said. "That woman below has told the janitor she is going to pour ammonia water down on my tomato plants tonight, and I am making a few small preparations."

SALVAGE

I

After Charlie Sands had gone to a training camp in Ohio there was a great change in Tish. She seemed for the first time to regret that she was a woman, and there were times when that wonderful poise and dignity that had always distinguished her, even under the most trying circumstances, almost deserted her. She wrote, I remember, a number of letters to the President, offering to go into the Secret Service, and sending a photograph of the bandits she had caught in Glacier Park. But she only received a letter from Mr. Tumulty in reply, commencing "May I not thank you," but saying that the Intelligence Department had recently been increased by practically the entire population of the country, and suggesting that she could best use her energies for the national welfare by working for the return of the Democratic Party in 1920.

However, as Tish is a Republican she was not interested in this, and for a time she worked valiantly for the Red Cross and spent her evenings learning the national anthem. But she recited it, since, as the well-known writer, Mr. Irvin Cobb, has observed, it can only be properly sung by a boy whose voice is changing. It was evident, however, that she was increasingly restive, and as I look back I wonder that we did not realize that there was danger in her very repression.

As Aggie has said, Tish is volcanic in her temperament; she remains inactive for certain preparatory periods, but when she overflows she does so thoroughly.

The most ominous sign was when, in July of 1917, she stopped knitting and took up French.

Only the other day, while house cleaning, she came across the aeroplane photograph of the French village of V — , where our extraordinary experience befell us, and she turned on us both with that satiric yet kindly gaze which we both knew so well.

"If you two idiots had had your way," she observed, "I should have been knitting so many socks for Charlie Sands that he'd have had to be a centipede to wear 'em all, instead of —"

"Tish," Aggie said in a shivering voice, "I wish you wouldn't talk about it. I can't bear it, that's all. It sets me shivering."

Tish eyed her coldly. "The body is entirely controlled by the mind, Aggie," she reminded her. "And when I remember how nearly your lack of control cost us our lives, when you insisted on sneezing —"

"Insisted! If you had been in a shell hole full of water up to your neck, Tish Carberry —"

"The difference between you and me, Aggie," Tish replied calmly, "is that I should not have been in a shell hole full of water up to my neck." The war was over then, of course, but there was still a disturbed condition in certain countries, and Tish's eyes grew reflective.

"I see they are thinking of sending a real army into Russia," she said thoughtfully. "I suppose that Russian laundress of the Ostermaiers' could teach a body to talk enough to get about with."

Shortly after that Aggie disappeared, and I found her later on in Tish's bathroom crying into a Turkish towel.

"I won't go, Lizzie," she said, "and that's flat! I've done my share, and if Tish Carberry thinks I am going to go through the rest of my life falling into shell holes and being potted at by all sort of strange men she can just think again. Besides that, I have been true to the memory of one man for a good many years, and I simply refuse to be kissed by any more of those immoral foreigners."

Aggie had in her youth been betrothed to a gentleman in the roofing business, who had met with an unfortunate accident, owing to having slipped on a tin gutter, without overshoes, one rainy day; and it is quite true that we had all been kissed by two French generals and a man in civilian clothes who had not even been introduced to us. But up to that time we had kept the osculatory incident a profound secret.

"Aggie," I said with sudden suspicion, "you haven't told Mrs. Ostermaier about that affair, have you?"

Aggie put down the towel and looked at me defiantly.

"I have, Lizzie," she said. "Not all of it, but some. She said she had gone to the moving pictures with the youngest girl, but that she had been obliged to take her away before it was over, owing to a picture from France of Tish's being kissed by a French general. She said that as soon as he had kissed her on one cheek she turned the other, and that she thinks the effect on Dolores was extremely bad."

It was a great shock to us all to learn that the incident of the town of V — had thus been made public, and that there was a moving picture of our being decorated, et cetera, going about the country. It is, I believe, quite usual to kiss the persons receiving the Croix de Guerre, even when of the masculine sex, and I know positively that Tish never saw that French general again.

However, in view of the unfortunate publicity I have decided to make this record of the actual incident of the French town of V — . For the story has got into the papers, and only yesterday Tish discovered that the pleasant young man who had been trying to sell her a washing machine was really a newspaper reporter in disguise.

Certain things are not true. We did not see or have any conversation with the former Emperor of the Germans; nor were any of us wounded, though Aggie got a piece of plaster in her right eye when a shell hit the church roof, and I was badly scratched by barbed wire. It is not true, either, that Aggie had her teeth knocked out by a German sentry. She unfortunately fell in the darkness and lost her upper set, and it was impossible to light a match in order to search for them.

It was, as I have said, in July of the first year of the war that both Aggie and I noticed the change in Tish. She grew moody and abstracted, and on two Sundays in succession she turned over her Sunday-school class to me and went for long walks into the country. Also, going to her apartment for Sunday dinner on, I believe, the second Sunday of the month we were startled to see the Andersons, very nice people who occupy the lower floor of the building, running out wildly into the street. They said that the janitor had been quarreling with some one in the furnace cellar, and that from high words, which they could plainly hear, they had got to shooting, and a bullet had come up through the floor and hit the phonograph.

I had a strange feeling at once, and I caught Aggie's agonized eyes on me. We remained for some time in the street, and then, everything seeming to be quiet, we ventured in, with two policemen leading the way, and the Anderson baby left outside in its perambulator for fear of accident. All was quiet, however, and we made our way upstairs to Tish's apartment. She was waiting for us, and reading the *Presbyterian Banner*, but I thought she was almost too calm when we told her of the Andersons' terrible experience.

"It's a good riddance," she said, referring to the phonograph. "Besides, what right have people over here to fuss about one bullet? Think of our boys in the trenches."

After a time she looked up suddenly and said: "It didn't go anywhere near the baby, I suppose?"

We said it had not, and she then observed that the building was a mere shell, and that people with small children should raise them in the country anyhow.

It was during dinner — Tish had been reading Horace Fletcher for some time, and meals lasted almost from one to the next — that Hannah came in and said the janitor wanted to see Tish. She went out and came back somewhat later, looking as irritated as our dear Tish ever looks, and got her pocketbook from behind the china closet and went out again.

"I expected as much," Hannah said. Hannah is Tish's maid. "She's paying blackmail. Like as not that janitor will collect a hundred dollars from her, and that phonograph never cost more than thirty-five. They're paying for it on the installment plan, and the man only gets a dollar a week."

"Hannah," I said sharply, "if you mean to insinuate —"

"Me?" Hannah replied in a hurt tone. "I don't insinuate anything. If I was called tomorrow before a judge and jury I'd say that for all I know Miss Tish was reading the *Banner* all morning. But I'd pray they wouldn't take a trip here and look in the upper right-hand sideboard drawer."

She then went out and slammed the door.

Aggie and I make it a point of honor never to pry into Tish's secrets, so we did not, of course, look into the drawer. However, a moment later I happened to upset my glass of water and naturally went to the sideboard drawer in question for a fresh napkin. And Tish's revolver was lying underneath her best monogrammed tray cover.

"It's there, Aggie," I said. "Her revolver. She's practicing again; and you know what that means — war."

Aggie gave a low moan.

"I wish we'd let her get that aeroplane. She might have been satisfied, Lizzie," she said in a shaken voice.

"She might have been dead too," I replied witheringly.

And then Tish came back. She said nothing about the Andersons; but later on when the baby started to cry she observed rather bitterly that she didn't see why people had to have a phonograph when they had that, and that personally she felt that whoever destroyed that phonograph should have a vote of thanks instead of — She did not complete the sentence.

It was soon after that that we went to visit Charlie Sands, Tish's nephew, at the camp where he was learning to be an officer. We called to see the colonel in command first, and Aggie gave him two extra blankets for Charlie Sands' bed and a pair of knitted bedroom slippers. He was very nice to us and promised to see personally that they went to the proper bed.

"I'm always delighted to attend to these little things," he said.

"Fine to feel that our boys are comfortable. You haven't by any chance brought an eiderdown pillow?"

He seemed very regretful when he found we had not thought of one.

"That's too bad," he said. "I've discovered that there is nothing so comforting as a down pillow after a day of strenuous labor."

It was rather disappointing to find that the duties of his position kept him closely confined to the office, and that therefore he had not yet had the pleasure of meeting Tish's nephew, but he said he had no doubt they would meet before long.

"They're all brought in here sooner or later, for one thing or another," he said pleasantly.

As Tish observed going out, it was pleasant to to think of Charlie Sands' being in such good hands.

It was, however, rather a shock to find him, when we did find him, lying on his stomach in a mud puddle with a rifle in front of him. We did not recognize him at once, as a lot of men were yelling, and indeed just at first he did not seem particularly glad to see us.

"Suffering cats!" he shouted. "Don't you see we're shooting? You'll be killed. Get behind the line!"

"I guess it won't defeat the Allies if you stop shooting for two minutes," Tish observed with her splendid poise. "But if you will take charge of this homemade apple butter, which I didn't trust your colonel with, we will go to your sitting room, or wherever it is you receive visitors."

There was quite a crowd of young officers round us by that time and we waited to be introduced. But Charlie Sands did not seem to think of it, so Tish put down the apple butter on the ground and said to one of them:

"Now, young man, since we seem to be in your way, perhaps you will take us to some place to wait for my nephew." Then seeing that he looked rather strange she added: "But perhaps you have never met. This is my nephew, Mr. Sands. If you will tell me who you are —"

"Williams is my name," he said. "I — Major Williams. I — I've met your nephew — that is — Private Sands, take these ladies to the Y. M. C. A. hut, and report back here in an hour."

Tish did not like this; nor did I. As Tish observed later, he might have been speaking to the butler.

"He might at least have said 'Mister,' and a 'please' hurts no one," she said. As for giving him only an hour when we had come a hundred miles — it was absurd. But war does queer things.

It had indeed strangely altered Tish's nephew. We were all worried about him that day. It was his manner that was odd. He seemed, as Tish said later, suppressed. When for instance we wished to take him back to headquarters and present him to the colonel he said at once: "Who? Me? The colonel! Say, you'd better get this and get it right: I'm nothing here. I'm less than nothing. Why, the colonel could walk right over me on the parade ground and never even know he'd stepped on anything. If I was a louse and he was a can of insect powder —"

"Now see here, Charlie Sands," Tish said firmly, "I'll trouble you to remember that there are certain words not in my vocabulary; and louse is one of them."

"Still, a vocabulary is a better place than some others I can think of," he observed.

"What is more," Tish added, "you are misjudging that charming colonel. He told us himself that he tried to be a mother to you all."

She then told him how interested the colonel had been in the blankets, and so on, but I must say Charlie Sands was very queer about it. He stopped and looked at us all in turn, and then he got out the dirtiest handkerchief I have ever seen and wiped his forehead with it.

"Perhaps you'd better say it again," he said; "I don't seem to get it altogether. You are sure it was the colonel?"

So Tish repeated it, but when she came to the eiderdown pillow he held up his hand.

"All right," he said in a strange tone. "I believe you. I — you don't mind if I go and get a drink of water, do you? My mouth is dry."

Dear Tish watched him as he went away, and shook her head.

"He is changed already," she observed sadly. "That is one of the deadliest effects of war. It takes the bright young spirit of youth and feeds it on stuff cooked by men, with not even time enough to chew properly, and puts it on its stomach in the mud, while its head is in the clouds of idealism. I think that a letter to the Secretary of War might be effective."

I must admit that we had a series of disappointments that day. The first was in finding that they had put Tish's nephew, a grandson of a former Justice of the Supreme Court, into a building with a number of other men. Not only that but without so much as a screen, or a closet in which to hang up his clothing.

"What do you mean, hang up my clothes?" he said when we

protested. "They're hung up all right — on me."

"It seems rather terrible," Aggie objected gently. "No privacy or anything."

"Privacy! I haven't got anything to hide."

We found some little comfort, however, in the fact that beneath the pitiful cot that he called his bed he had a small tin trunk. Even that was destroyed, however, by the entrance of a thin young man called Smithers, who reached under the cot and dragging out the trunk proceeded to take out one of the pairs of socks that Aggie had knitted.

Charlie Sands paid no attention, but Tish fixed this person with a cold eye.

"Haven't you made a mistake?" she inquired. The young man was changing his socks, with his back to us, and he looked back over his shoulder.

"Sorry!" he said. "Didn't like to ask you to go out. Haven't any place else to go, you know."

"Aren't you putting on my nephew's socks?"

"Extraordinary!" he said. "Did you notice that?"

"I'll trouble you to take them off, young man."

"Well," he said reflectively, "I'll tell you what we'll do: I'll take off these socks if he'll return what he's got on that belongs to me. I don't remember exactly, but I'm darn sure of his underwear and his breeches. You see, while you good people at home are talking democracy we're practicing it, and Sands' idea is the best yet. He swaps an entire outfit for a pair of socks. Even the Democratic Party can't improve on that."

Tish was very thoughtful during the remainder of the afternoon, but she brightened somewhat when, later on, we sat on the steps of a building watching Charlie Sands and a number of others going through what Major Williams called setting-up exercises. She was greatly interested and made notes in her memorandum book. I have a copy of the book before me now. The letter T, S, A and B stand respectively for Toes, Stomach, Arms and Back. I shall not quote all Tish's notes, but this one, for instance, is illustrative of her thorough methods:

> "Lying on B. in mud, H. flat on ground, L. rigidly extended: Rise L. in air six times. Retaining prone position rise to sitting position without aid of A., but using S. muscles. Repeat six times. [Note: Director uses language unfitting a soldier and a gentleman. Report to the Secretary of War.]"

She recorded the other movements with similar care, and after one is the thoughtful observation: "Excellent to make Lizzie look less like a bolster."

I find all of Tish's notes taken that day as very indicative of the thoroughness with which she does everything. For instance she made the following recommendations to be sent to the War Department:

> "That the camp cooks be instructed to use hemmed tea towels instead of sacking, and to boil the dish towels after each meal, preferably with soap powder and soda.
>
> "That screens be provided between cots, to give that measure of privacy necessary to a man's self-respect.
>
> "Large, commodious clothes closets in the barracks. A bag of camphor in each one would serve to keep away moths. Also, that wearing apparel should not be borrowed.
>
> "All army blankets should be marked as to the end to go to the top of the cot. Sheets should also be provided, as blankets scratch and have a tendency to keep the soldier awake.
>
> "Soda fountains here and there through the camp would do a great deal to prevent the men in training from going to neighboring towns after certain deleterious liquids. [Should, however, be served by male attendants.]
>
> "Pyjamas should be included in every soldier's equipment. [Charlie Sands had told us a startling thing. On inquiring what had become of the raw-silk pyjamas we had made him as a part of his army equipment he confessed that he did not use them, and in fact had torn them into rags to clean his gun. He went even further, and stated that it was not the custom of the men to use pyjamas at all, and that in fact on cold nights some of them merely removed their hats and shoes, and then retired.]
>
> "Table linen, even if coarse, should be provided. Are our men to come back to us savages?"

It may have been purely coincidence, but soon after Tish's recommendations had been received at the War Department the Fosdick Commission was appointed. Yet we carried away a conviction that though certain things had been sadly neglected Charlie Sands was in good hands. The colonel came up to speak to us when, seeing the men standing in rows on the parade ground about sunset while the band played, we stood watching.

He was very pleasant, and said that they were about to bring in the flag. Some such conversation then ensued:

Tish: Do you bring in the flag every night?

The Colonel: Every night, madam.

Tish: Then you are a better housekeeper than I thought you were.

The Colonel: I beg your pardon?

Tish (magnanimously): You may not know much about dish-cloths, but you are right about flags. They do fade, and I dare say dew is about as bad as rain for them.

He seemed very much gratified by her approval, and said in twenty-five years in the Army he had never failed to have the flag brought in at night. "I may fail in other things," he said wistfully. "To err is human, you know. But the flag proposition is one I stand pat on."

It was after our return visit to the camp that the real change in Tish began. We had gone to our cottage in Lake Penzance for the summer, and Tish suggested that we study French there. She had an excellent French book, with photographs in it showing where to place the tongue and how to pucker the lips for certain sounds. At first she did not allow us to do anything but practice these facial expressions, and I remember finding Hannah in the kitchen one night crying into her bread sponge and asking her what the trouble was.

"I just can't bear it, Miss Lizzie," she said; "when I look in and see the three of you sitting there making faces I nearly go crazy. I've got so I do it myself, and the milkman won't leave the bottles no nearer than the gate."

After some days of silent practice Tish considered that we could advance a lesson, and we began with syllable sounds, thus:

> *Ba* — Said with tip of tongue against lower teeth.
> *Be* — Show two upper middle teeth.
> *Bi* — Broad smile.
> *Bu* — Whistle.
> *Bon* — Pout.

It was an excellent method, though we all found difficulty in showing only two upper middle teeth.

There were also syllables which called for hollow cheeks, and I remember Tish's irritation at my failure.

"If you would eat less whipped cream, Lizzie," she said scathingly, "you might learn the French language. Otherwise you might as well give it up."

"I dare say there are plump people among the French," I retorted. "And I never heard that a Frenchwoman who put on twenty pounds or so went dumb. That woman who trims your hats isn't dumb so you could notice it. I'd thank my stars if she was. She can say forty dollars fast enough, and she doesn't suck in her cheeks either!"

In the end Aggie and I gave up the French lessons, but Tish kept them up. She learned ten nouns a day, and she made an attempt at verbs, but gave it up.

"I can secure anything I want, if I ever visit our valiant Ally," she said, "by naming it in the French and then making the appropriate gesture."

She made the experiment on Hannah, and it worked well enough. She would say "butter" or "spoon" and point to her place at the table; but Hannah almost left on the strength of it, and when she tried it on Mr. Jennings, the fishman, he told all over Penzance that she had lost either her mind or her teeth.

Aggie and I were extremely uneasy all of July, for Tish does nothing without a motive, and she was learning in French such warlike phrases as "Take the trenches," "The enemy is retiring," and "We must attack from the rear." She also took to testing out the engine of her automobile in various ways, and twice, trying to cross a plowed field with it, had to be drawn out with a rope. She took to driving at night without lights also, and had the ill luck to run into the Penzance doctor's buggy and take a wheel off it.

It was after that incident, when we had taken the doctor home and put him to bed, that I demanded an explanation.

But she only said with a far-away look in her eyes: "It may be a useful accomplishment sometime. If one were going after wounded at night it would be invaluable."

"Not if you killed all the doctors on the way!" I snapped.

The limit to our patience came soon after that. One morning about the first of August the boatman from the lake came up the path with a spade over his shoulder. Tish, we perceived, tried to take him aside, but he gave her no time.

"Well, I've done it, Miss Tish," he said, "and God only knows what'll happen if somebody runs into it between now and tomorrow morning."

"Nobody will know you did it unless you continue to shout the way you are doing now."

"Oh, I'll not tell," he observed; "I'm not so proud of it. But 'twouldn't surprise me a mite if we both did some time together in the county jail, on the head of it, Miss Tish."

Well, Aggie went pale, but Tish merely gave him five dollars and spent the rest of the day shut in the garage with her car. I went back and looked in the window during the afternoon, and she was on her back under it, hammering at something.

That night at dinner she made an announcement.

"I have for some time," she said, "been considering — go out, Hannah, and close the door — been considering the values of different engines for an ambulance which I propose to take to France."

"Tish!" Aggie cried in a heart-rending tone.

"And I have come to the conclusion that my own car has the best engine on the market. Tonight I propose to make a final test and if it succeeds I shall have an ambulance body built on it. I know this engine; I may almost say I have an affection for it. And it has served me well. Why, I ask you, should I abandon it and take some new-fangled thing that would as like as not lie down and die the minute it heard the first shell?"

"Exactly," I said with some feeling; "why should you, when you can count on me doing it anyhow?"

She ignored that, however, and said she had fully determined to go abroad and to get as near the Front as possible. She said also that she had already written General Pershing, and that she expected to start the moment his reply came.

"I told him," she observed, "that I would prefer not being assigned to any particular part of the line, as it was my intention, though not sacrificing the national good to it, to remain as near my nephew as possible. Pershing is a father and I felt that he would understand."

She then prepared to take the car out, and with a feeling of desperation Aggie and I followed her.

For some time we pursued the even tenor of our way, varied only by Tish's observing over her shoulder: "No matter what happens, do not be alarmed, and don't yell!"

Aggie was for getting out then, but we have always stood by Tish in an emergency, and we could not fail her then. She had turned into a dark lane and we were moving rapidly along it.

"When I say 'Ready!' brace yourselves for a jar," Tish admonished us. Aggie was trembling, and she had just put a small flash of blackberry cordial to her lips to steady herself when the machine went over the edge of a precipice, throwing Aggie into the road and myself forward into the front of the car.

There was complete silence for a moment. Then Aggie said in

a reproachful voice: "You didn't say 'Ready!' Tish."

Tish, however, said nothing, and in the starlight I perceived her bent forward over the steering wheel. The car was standing on its forward end at the time.

"Tish!" I cried. "Tish!"

She then straightened herself and put both hands over the pit of her stomach.

"I've burst something, Lizzie," she said in a strangled tone. "My gall bladder, probably."

She then leaned back and closed her eyes. We were greatly alarmed, as it is unlike our brave Tish to give in until the very last, but finally she sat erect, groaning.

"I am going back and kill that boatman," she said. "I told him to dig a shell hole, not a cellar." Here she stood up and felt her pulse. "If I've burst anything," she announced a moment later, "it's a corset steel. That boatman is a fool, but at least he has given us a chance to see if we are of the material which France requires at this tragic juncture."

"I can tell you right away that I am not," Aggie said tartly. "I'm not and I don't want to be. Though I can't see how biting my tongue half through is going to help France anyhow."

But Tish was not listening. She had lifted three shovels out of the car, and we could see her dauntless figure outlined against the darkness.

"The Germans," she said at last, "are over there behind that chicken house. The machine is stalled in a shell hole and contains a wounded soldier. We are being shelled and there are those what-you-call-'em lights overhead. We must escape or be killed. There is only one thing to do. Lizzie, what is your idea of the next step?"

"Anybody but a lunatic would know that," I said tartly. "The thing to do is to go home and make an affidavit that we never saw that car, and that the hole in this road is where it was struck by lighting."

"Aggie," Tish said without paying any attention to me, "here is a shovel for you."

But Aggie sniffed.

"Not at all, Tish Carberry," she observed. "I am the wounded soldier, and I don't stir a foot."

In the end, however, we all went to work to dig the car out of the hole, and at three o'clock in the morning Tish climbed in and started the engine. It climbed out slowly, but as Tish observed it gave an excellent account of itself.

"And I must say," she said, "I believe we have all shown that we can meet emergency in the proper spirit. As for the hole, that driveling idiot who dug it can fill it up tomorrow morning and no one be the wiser."

I have made this explanation because of the ugly reports spread by the boatman himself. It is necessary, because it appears that he became intoxicated on the money Tish had so generously given him, and the milk wagon which supplied us going into the hole an hour or so after we had left he shamelessly told his own part and ours in the catastrophe. The result was that waking the next morning with a severe attack of lumbago I heard our splendid Tish being attacked verbally by the milkman and forced to pay an outrageous sum in damages.

By September Tish had had the old body removed from her automobile and an ambulance body built on. She made the drawings for it herself, and it contained many improvements over the standard makes. It contained, for instance, a cigarette lighter — not that Tish smokes, but because wounded men always do, and we knew that matches were scarce in France. It also contained an ice-water tank, a reading lamp, with a small portable library of improving books selected by our clergyman, Mr. Ostermaier, and a false bottom. This last Tish was rather mysterious about, merely remarking that it might be a good place for Aggie to retire to if she took a sneezing spell within earshot of the enemy.

When I look back and recall how foresighted Letitia Carberry was I am filled with admiration of those sterling qualities which have so many times brought us safely out of terrible danger.

We were, however, doomed at first to real disappointment. With everything arranged, with the ambulance ready and our costumes made, we could not get to France. Tish made a special trip to Washington to see the Secretary of War, and he remembered very well her recommendations as to the camps, and so forth, and said that he had referred the matter of pyjamas, for instance, to the Chief of Staff. He himself felt that the point was well taken. He believed in pyjamas, and wore them, but that he had an impression, though he did not care to go on record about it, that the chief of staff advocated nightshirts. He also said that he had a letter from General Pershing asking that no relatives of soldiers go to France, as he was afraid that the gentle and restraining influence of their loved ones would impair their taste for war.

Aggie and I began to have a little hope at that time, and Aggie tore up a will she had made leaving her property to the Red Cross, on condition that it kept up Mr. Wiggins' lot in the cemetery. But just as we were feeling more cheerful Aggie had a warning. She had been reading everywhere of the revival in spiritualism, and once before when she was in doubt she had been most successful with a woman who told the future with the paste letters that are used in soup. She went to a clairvoyant and he told her to be very careful of high places, and that the warning came from some one who had passed over from a high place. He thought it was an aviator, but we knew better, and Aggie looked at me with agonized eyes.

Aggie has said since that when she was in her terrible position at V — she remembered that warning, but of course it was too late then.

It was when we had gone back to the city that we realized that Tish was still determined to get to France. Only two days after our return she came in with a book called "Military Codes and Signals," and gave it to Aggie. She had it marked at a place which told how to signal at night with an electric flashlight, and from that time on for several weeks she would sit in her window at night, with Aggie on the pavement across the street, also with a pocket flash, both of them signaling anything that came into their heads. It was rather hard on Aggie on cold evenings, and I remember very well that one night she came in and threw her flashlight on the floor, and then burst into tears.

"I'm through, Tish," she said, "and that's all there is to it! I've stood being frozen until my feet are so cold I can't tell one from the other, but I draw the line at being insulted."

"Insulted?" Tish said. "If you are going to mind trifles when your country's safety is in question you'd better stay at home. Who insulted you?"

Well, it seems that by way of conversation Aggie had flashed that the wretch with the cornet who rooms above Tish's apartment was at the window watching and she wished he'd fall out and break his neck.

He had then put out his own light and had appeared in the window again, and had flashed in the same code: "Come, birdie, fly with me."

For certain reasons I have decided not to reveal how Tish finally arranged that we should get to France. As the Secretary of War says, it might make him very unpopular with the many women he had been obliged to refuse. It is enough to say that the wonderful day finally came when we found ourselves on the very ocean which had carried Tish's nephew on his glorious mission. Aggie was particularly exalted as we went down the bay, escorted by encircling aeroplanes.

"I'm not a brave woman, Tish," she said softly, "but as I look back on that glorious sky line I feel that no sacrifice is too great to make for it. I am ready to do or die."

"Humph," said Tish. "Well, as far as I'm concerned, after the prices they charged me at that hotel the Germans are welcome to New York. I'd give it to them and say 'Thank you' when they took it."

We then went below and tried on our life-preserving suits, which the clerk at the steamship office had rented to us at fifteen dollars each.

He said they were most essential, and that when properly inflated one could float about in them for a week. Indeed, as Tish said, with a compass and a small sail one could probably make the nearest land, such as the Azores, supporting life in the meantime with ship's biscuits, and so on, in waterproof packages, carried in the pockets provided for the purpose. She did indeed go so far as to place a bottle of blackberry cordial in the pocket of each suit, and also a small tin of preserved ginger, which we have always found highly sustaining. But we were somewhat uneasy to discover that it required a considerable length of time to get into the suits.

We had barely got into them when we heard a bugle blowing and men running. Just after that an alarm bell began to ring, and Aggie said "It has come!" and as usual commenced to sneeze violently. We ran out on deck, dear Tish saying to be calm, as more lives were lost through excitement than anything else; though she herself was none too calm, for when we found afterward that it was only a lifeboat drill I discovered that she was carrying her silver-handled umbrella.

Every one was on the deck, and I must say that we were followed by envious glances. As we had inflated the suits they were not immodest, effectually concealing the lines of the figure, but making it difficult to pass through doorways.

There was a very nice young man on deck, in a Red Cross uniform, and he said that as he was the only male in our lifeboat he was pleased to see that three of the eighteen ladies in it were prepared to take care of themselves. He said that he felt he would probably have his hands full saving the fifteen others.

"Not," he added, "that I should feel comfortable until you were safely in the boat anyhow. I should not like to think of you floating about, perhaps for weeks, and possibly dodging sharks and so on."

Tish liked him at once, and said that in case of trouble if the boat were crowded we would only ask for a towing line.

It was while this conversation was going on that Aggie suddenly said: "I've changed my mind, Tish, I'm not going."

Well, we looked at her. She was a green color, and she said she'd thank us to put her off in something or other and let her go back. She wasn't seasick, but she just didn't care for the sea. She never had and she never would. And then she said "Ugh!" and the Red Cross man put his arm around her as far as it would go in the rubber suit, and said that certainly she was not seasick, but that some people found the sea air too stimulating, and she'd better go below and not get too much of it at first.

He helped us get Aggie down to her cabin, but unluckily he put her down on Tish's knitting. We had the misfortune to hear a slow hissing sound, and her inflated suit began to wilt immediately, where a steel needle had penetrated it.

Even then both Tish and I noticed that he had a sad face, and later on, when we had put Aggie to bed in her life suit, for she refused to have it taken off, we sat in Tish's cabin across, listening to Aggie's moans and to his story.

Tish had immediately demanded to know why he was not in the uniform of a fighting man, and he said at once: "I'm glad you asked me that. I've been wanting to tell the whole ship about it, but it's so darned ridiculous. I've tried every branch and they've all turned me down, for a — for a physical infirmity."

"Flat feet?" Tish asked.

"No. The truth is, I've had a milk leg. Fact. I know it is — er — generally limited to the other sex at — er — certain periods. But I've had it. Can't hike any distance. Can't run. Couldn't even kick a Hun," he added bitterly. "And what's more, there's a girl on this ship who thinks I'm a slacker, and I can't tell her about it. She wouldn't believe me if I did — though why a fellow would make up a milk leg I don't know. And she'd laugh. Everybody laughs. I've made a lot of people happy."

"Why don't you tell her you have heart disease?" Tish inquired in a gentler tone. Though not young herself she has preserved a fine interest in the love affairs of youth.

"Oh, I've got that all right," he said gloomily. "But it's not the sort that keeps a fellow out of the Army. It's — well, that doesn't matter. But suppose I told her that? She wouldn't marry me with heart disease."

"Tish!" Aggie called faintly.

In the end we were obliged to cut the rubber suit off with the scissors, as she not only refused to get up but wanted to drown if we were torpedoed. We therefore did not see the young man again until evening, and then he was with a very pretty girl in a Y. M. C. A. uniform. We had gone up on deck for air, and Tish was looking for the captain. She had a theory that if we could put Aggie in a hammock she would feel better, as the hammock would remain stationary while the ship rocked. Just as we passed them, the girl said: "He's the best-looking man on the ship anyhow. And he's a captain in the infantry. He says it is the most dangerous branch of the service."

"Oh, he does, does he?" said the Red Cross young man. "Well, you'd better wait six months before you fall too hard for him. He may get his face changed, and there isn't much behind it."

He spoke quite savagely, and both Tish and I felt that he was making a mistake, and that gentleness, with just a suggestion of the caveman beneath, would have been more efficacious. Indeed when we knew Mr. Burton better — that was his name — we ventured the suggestion, but he only shook his head.

"You don't know her," he said. "She is the sort of girl who likes to take the soft-spoken fellow and make him savage. And when she gets the cave type she wants to tame him. I've tried being both, so I know. I'm damned — I beg your pardon — I'm cursed if I know why I care for her. I suppose it's because she has about as much use for me as she has for a dose of Paris green. But if you hear of that Weber who hangs round her going overboard some night, I hope you'll understand. That's all."

That conversation, however, was later on in the voyage. That first night out Tish saw the captain and he finally agreed, if we said nothing about it, to have a sailor's hammock hung in Aggie's cabin.

"It wouldn't do to have it get about, madam," he said. "You know how it is — I'd have all the passengers in hammocks in twenty-four hours, and the crew sleeping on the decks. And you know crews are touchy these days, what with submarines and chaplains and young shave-tails of officers who expect to be kissed every time they're asked to get off a coil of rope."

We promised secrecy, and that evening a hammock was hung in Aggie's cabin. It was not much like a hammock, however, and it was so high that Tish said it looked more like a chandelier than anything else. Getting Aggie into it required the steward, the stewardess, Mr. Burton and ourselves, but it was finally done, and we all felt easier at once, except that I was obliged to stand on a chair to feed her her beef tea.

However, just after midnight Tish and I in our cabin across

heard a terrible thud, followed by silence and then by low, dreadful moans. Aggie had fallen out. She did not speak at all for some time, and when she did it was to horrify Tish. For she said: "Damnation!"

Tish immediately turned and left the cabin, leaving me to press a cold knife against the lump on Aggie's head and to put her back into her berth. She refused the hammock absolutely. She said she had forgotten where she was, and had merely reached out for her bedroom slippers, which were six feet below, when the whole thing had turned over and thrown her out.

She insisted that she did not remember saying anything improper, but that the time Tish's horse had thrown her in the cemetery she had certainly used strong language, to say the least.

I remember telling Tish this, and she justified herself by the subconscious mind, which she was studying at the time. She said that the subconscious mind stored up all the wicked words and impulses which the conscious mind puts virtuously from it. And she recalled the fact that Mr. Ostermaier, our clergyman, taking laughing gas to have a tooth drawn, tried to kiss the dentist on coming out, and called him a sweet little thing — though Mrs. Ostermaier is quite a large woman.

We became quite friendly with Mr. Burton during the remainder of the voyage. He formed the habit of coming down every evening before dinner to our cabin and having a dose of blackberry cordial to prevent seasickness.

"I've had it before," he said on one occasion, "but never with such — er — medicinal qualities. You don't put anything in it but blackberries, do you?"

"Only a little alcohol to preserve it," I told him with some pride. I generally make it myself.

"I will say this for it: It's extremely well preserved," he said, and filled up the tooth mug again. It was after that that he told us that Hilda had refused to marry him, and was flirting outrageously with Captain Weber.

"I only say this," he added gloomily: "He's right when he says he belongs in the infantry. He's got the photographs of five youngsters in his cabin; or he did have. He's probably hidden them now."

"Why don't you tell her?" Tish demanded.

"Why should I? Let her make a fool of herself if she wants to," he said despondently. "What chance have I against a shipload of 'em, anyhow? If it wasn't this one it would be another. She's got her eye on a tank now, and she's only waiting for that aviator to forget his stomach to sit at his feet and worship. God only knows what would happen if we had a Croix de Guerre on board."

He sat for some time, sipping the blackberry cordial and looking into space.

"I've got it figured out this way," he said at last. "I've got to pull off something over there. That's all. Got to get in the papers and get a medal and a wooden leg. She'd stand for a wooden leg better than a milk one," he added viciously.

Both Aggie and I noticed that Tish regarded him with a contemplative eye, and from, that time on she spent at least a part of every day with him. He paid no attention at all to Hilda from that time on, and one morning while Tish and Mr. Burton were walking by her chair she dropped a book. But he did not seem to see it, and that evening the captain moved over to her table, and Mr. Burton was very gay, but ate hardly any dinner.

We all went in the same train to Paris, and he had a sort of revenge then. For the captain could not speak French, and she had to ask Mr. Burton to order her dinner for her. But he ordered only one, and the captain was furious, naturally.

"Look here, Burton," he said, "I'm here, you know."

"Why, so you are," said Mr. Burton coldly. "I hadn't noticed you."

"How the devil can I make that woman understand that I'm hungry?"

Mr. Burton reflected.

"I'll tell you," he said. "You might open your mouth and point down your throat. Most of these French know the sign language."

He turned away then, and I saw a gleam of triumph in Tish's eye. She leaned over to him.

"She's furious that he can't speak French," she said. "Talk to me in French, and don't mind what I say. The only thing I can remember is a list of a hundred nouns. I'll string them together somehow."

There was a French officer near us, and I saw him watching Tish carefully as the conversation went on. She said afterward that as near as she could make out, Mr. Burton was telling the history of the country we went through, and that when he paused she would say in French: "Handkerchief, fish, trunk, pencil, book, soup," or some such list.

But it impressed Hilda; I could see that.

It was some time before we got out of Paris, and the news we had of Charlie Sands was that he was at the Front, near V — , which was held by the enemy. Tish went out and bought a map, and decided that she would be sent in that direction or nowhere. But for several weeks nothing happened, and she found the ambulance had come and was being used to carry ice cream to convalescent hospitals round Paris. What was more, she could not get it back.

For once I thought our dauntless Tish was daunted. How true it is that we forget past success in present failure! But after a number of mysterious absences she came into my room after Aggie had gone to bed and said: "I've found where they keep it."

"Keep what?"

"My ambulance."

I was putting my hair on wavers at the time, and I saw in the mirror that she had her hat and coat on, and the expression she wears when she has decided to break the law.

"I'm not going to spend this night in a French jail, Tish Carberry," I said.

"Very well," she retorted, and turned to go out.

But the thought of Tish alone, embarked on a dangerous enterprise, was too much for me, and I called her back.

"I'll go," I said, "and I'll steal, if that's what you're up to. But I'm a fool, and I know it. You can't deceive a lot of Frenchmen with your handkerchief-fish-trunk-pencil stuff. And you can't book-soup-oysters yourself out of jail."

"I'm taking my own, and only my own," Tish said with dignity.

Well, I dressed and we went out into the street. I tried to tell Tish that even if we got it we couldn't take it home and hide it under the bed or in a bureau drawer, but she was engrossed in her own thoughts, and besides, the streets were entirely dark and not a taxicab anywhere. She had a city map, however, and a flashlight, and at last about two in the morning we reached the street where she said it was stored in a garage.

I was limping by that time, and there were cold chills running up and down my spine, but Tish was quite calm. And just then there was a terrific outburst of noise, whistles and sirens of all sorts, and a man walking near us suddenly began to run and dived into a doorway.

"Air raid," said Tish calmly, and walked on. I clutched at her arm, but she shook me off.

"Tish!" I begged.

"Don't be a craven, Lizzie," she said. "Statistics show that the percentage of mortality from these things is considerably less than from mumps, and not to be compared with riding in an elevator or with the perils of maternity."

All sorts of people were running madly by that time, and suddenly disappearing, and a man with a bird cage in his hand bumped flat into me and knocked me down. Tish, however, had moved on without noticing, and when I caught up to her she was standing beside a wide door which was open, staring in.

"This is the place," she said. And just then half a dozen men poured out through the doorway and ran along the street. Tish drew a long breath.

"You see?" she said. "Providence watches over those whose motives are pure, even if compelled to certain methods —"

There was a terrible crash at that moment down the street, followed by glass falling all round us.

" — which are not entirely ethical," Tish continued calmly. "We might as well go inside, Lizzie. They may drop another, and we shall never have such a chance again."

"I can't walk, Tish," I said in a quavering voice. "My knees are bending backward."

"Fiddlesticks!" she replied scornfully and stalked inside.

I have since reflected on Tish during that air raid, on the calm manner in which she filled the gasoline tank of her ambulance, on the way in which she flung out six empty ice-cream freezers, and the perfect aplomb with which she kicked the tires to see if they contained sufficient air. For such attributes I have nothing but admiration. But I am not so certain as to the mental processes which permitted her calmly to take three spare tires from other cars and to throw them into the ambulance.

Perhaps there is with all true greatness an element of ruthlessness. Or perhaps she subsequently sent conscience money to the Red Cross anonymously. There are certain matters on which I do not interrogate her.

I was still sitting on the running board of a limousine inhaling my smelling salts when she pronounced all ready and we got into the driving seat and started. Just as we moved out a man came in from the street and began to yell at us. When Tish paid no attention to him he took a flying leap and landed on the step beside us.

"Here, what the — do you think you are doing?" he said in English. "Where's your permit?"

Tish said nothing, but turned out into the street and threw on the gas. He was on my side and the jerk almost flung him off.

"Stop this car!" he yelled. "Hey, Grogan! Grogan!"

But whoever Grogan was he was still in some cellar probably, and by that time we were going very fast. Unluckily the glass in the street cut all four tires almost immediately, and we swung madly from one side to the other. And just then, too, we struck the hole the shell had made, and went into it with a terrible bump. The man disappeared immediately, but Tish was quite composed. She simply changed gears, and the car crawled out on the other side.

"This motor will go anywhere, Lizzie," she said easily. "I feel that my judgment is entirely vindicated. Where's that man?"

"Killed, probably," I retorted with a certain acidity.

"I hope not," she replied with kindly tolerance. "But if he is it will be supposed that a bomb did it."

As a matter of fact the *Herald* next morning reported the miraculous escape of an American found on the very edge of a shell hole, recovering, but showing one of the curious results of shell shock, being convinced that two women had stolen a car from his garage, and had run it into the hole in a deliberate attempt to kill him.

Aggie read this to us at breakfast, and Tish merely observed that it was very sad, and that she proposed studying shell shock at the Front. Not until months later did we tell Aggie the story of that night.

That morning Tish disappeared, and at noon she came back to say that she had at last secured the ambulance, and that we would start for the Front at once. Privately she told me that in a pocket of the car she had found permits to get us out of Paris, but that the car would be missed before long, and that we would better start at once.

It is strange to look back and recall with what blitheness we prepared to leave. And it is interesting, too, to remember the conversation with Mr. Burton when he called that afternoon.

"Hello!" he said, glancing about. "This looks like moving on. Where to, oh, brave and radiant spirits?"

"We haven't quite decided," Tish said. She was cleaning her revolver at the time.

"You haven't decided! Great Scott, haven't you any orders? Or any permits?"

"All that are necessary," Tish said, squinting into the barrel of her revolver. "Aggie, don't forget your hay-fever spray."

"But look here," he began, "you know this is France in wartime. I hate to throw a wrench into the machinery, but no one can travel a mile in this country without having about a million papers. You'll be arrested; you'll be —"

"Young man," Tish said quietly, pouring oil on a rag, "I was arrested before you were born. Aggie, will you order some tea?

And make mine very weak."

"Weak tea!" he repeated with a sort of groan. "Weak tea! And yet you start for the Front, picking out any trench that takes your fancy, and — weak tea! And I am going to St.-Nazaire! I, a man, with a man's stomach and a mad affection for a girl who thinks I prefer serving doughnuts to fighting! I do that, while you —"

"Why do you go to St.-Nazaire?" Tish inquired. "You can sit with Aggie inside the ambulance, and I'm sure you could be useful, changing tires, and so on. You could simply disappear, you know. That is what we intend to do."

"I'll have a cup of tea," he said in a strange voice. "Very strong, please; I seem rather dazed."

"I figure this way," Tish went on, putting down her revolver and taking up her knitting: "I don't believe an ambulance loaded with cigarettes and stick candy and chocolate, with perhaps lemons for lemonade, is going to be stopped anywhere as long as it's headed for the Front. I understand they don't stop ambulances anyhow. If they do you can stretch out and pretend to be wounded. This is one way in which you can be very useful — being wounded."

He took all his tea at a gulp, and then looked round in an almost distracted manner.

"Certainly," he said. "Of course. It's all perfectly simple. You — you don't mind, I suppose, if I take a moment to arrange my mind? It seems to be all mussed up. Apparently I think clearly, but somehow or other —"

"We are actuated by several motives," Tish went on, beginning to turn the heel of the sock. "First of all, my nephew is at the Front. I want to be near him. I am a childless woman, and he is all I have. Second, I fancy the more cigarettes and so on our boys have the better for them, though I disapprove of cigarettes generally. And finally, I do not intend to let the biggest thing in my lifetime go by without having been a part of it, even in the most humble manner."

"Entirely reasonable too," he said.

But he still had a strange expression on his face, and soon after that he said he'd walk round a little in the air and then come back and tell us his decision.

At five o'clock he was back and he was very pale and wore what Aggie considered a haunted look. He stalked in and stood, his cap in his hand.

"I'll go," he said. "I'll go, and I don't give a — I don't care whether I come back or not. That's clear, isn't it? I'll go as far as you will, Miss Tish, and I take it that means moving right along. I'll go there, and then I'll keep on going."

"You've seen Hilda!" Aggie exclaimed with the intuition of her own experience in matters of the heart.

"I've seen her," he said grimly. "I wasn't looking for her. I've given that up. She was with that — well, you know. If I had any sense I'd have stolen those photographs and mailed them to her, one at a time. Five days, one each day, I'd have —"

"You might save all that hate for the Germans," Tish said. "I don't care to promise anything, but I have an idea that you may have a chance to use it."

And again, as always, our dear Tish was right.

We left Paris that evening. We made up quite comfortable beds in the ambulance, which had four new tires and which Tish with her customary forethought had filled as full as possible with cigarettes and candy. I have never inquired as to where Tish secured these articles, but I have learned that very early Tish adopted an army term called salvage, which seems to consist of taking whatever is necessary wherever it may be found. For instance, she has always referred to the night when she salvaged the ambulance and the extra tires; and the night later on, when we found the window of a warehouse open and secured seven cases of oranges for some of our boys who had no decent drinking water, she also referred to our actions at that time as salvage.

In fact, so common did the term become that I have heard her speaking of the time we salvaged the town of V — .

In re the matter of passports — *in re* is also military, and means referring to, or concerning; I find a certain tendency myself to use military terms. *In re* the matter of passports and permits, since the authenticity of our adventure has recently been challenged here at home, particularly in our church, though we have been lifelong members, it is a strange fact that we never required any. The sacred emblem on the ambulance and ourselves, including Mr. Burton, was amply sufficient. And though there were times when Mr. Burton found it expedient to lie in the back of the car and emit slow and tortured groans I have always contended that it was not really necessary in the two months which followed.

Over those two months I shall pass lightly. Our brave Tish was almost incessantly at the wheel, and we distributed uncounted numbers of cigarettes and so on. We had, naturally, no home other than the ambulance, but owing to Tish's forethought we found, among other articles in the secret compartment under the floor, a full store of canned goods and a nest of cooking kettles.

With this outfit we were able to supplement when necessary such provisions as we purchased along the way, and even now and then to make such occasional delicacies as cup custard or to bake a few muffins or small sweet cakes. More than once, too, we have drawn up beside the road where troops were passing, and turned out some really excellent hot doughnuts for them.

Indeed I may say that we became quite well known among both officers and men, being called The Three Graces.

But when so many were doing similar work on a much larger scale our poor efforts are hardly worthy of record. Only one thing is significant! We moved slowly but inevitably toward the Front, and toward that portion of the Front where Charlie Sands was serving his country.

During all this time Mr. Burton never mentioned Hilda but once, and that was to state that he had learned Captain Weber was a widower.

"Not that it makes any difference to me," he said. "She can marry him tomorrow as far as I'm concerned. I've forgotten her, practically. If I marry it will be one of these French girls. They can cook anyhow, and she can't. Her idea of a meal is a plate of fudge."

"He's really breaking his heart for her," Aggie confided to me later. "Do you notice how thin he is? And every time he looks at the moon he sighs."

"So do I," I said tartly; "and I'm not in love either. Ever since that moonlight night when that fool of a German flew over and dropped a bomb onto the best layer cake I've ever baked I've sighed at the moon too."

But he was thinner; and, when the weather grew cold and wet and we suggested flannels to him as delicately as possible, he refused to consider them.

"I'd as soon have pneumonia as not," he said. "It's quick and easy, and — anyhow we need them to cover the engine on cold nights."

It was, I believe, at the end of the seventh week that we drew in one night at a small village within sound of the guns. We limped in, indeed, for we had had one of our frequent blowouts, and had no spare tire.

Scattering as was our custom, we began a search for an extra tire, but without results. There was only one machine in the town, and that belonged to General Pershing. We knew it at once by the four stars. As we did not desire to be interrogated by the commander-in-chief we drew into a small alleyway behind a ruined house, and Aggie and I cooked a Spanish omelet and arranged some lettuce-and-mayonnaise sandwiches.

Tish had not returned, but Mr. Burton came back just as I was placing the meal on the folding table we carried for the purpose, and we saw at once that something was wrong. He wore a look he had not worn since we left Paris.

"Leg, probably," I said in an undertone to Aggie. He was subject to attacks of pain in the milk leg.

But Aggie's perceptions were more tender.

"Hilda, most likely," she said.

However, we were distracted by the arrival of Tish, who came in with her customary poise and unrolled her dinner napkin with a thoughtful air. She commented kindly on the omelet, but was rather silent.

At the end of the meal, however, she said: "If you will walk up the road past the Y. M. C. A. hut, Mr. Burton, it is just possible you will find an extra tire lying there. I am not positive, but I think it likely. I should continue walking until you find it."

"Must have seen a rubber plant up that way," Mr. Burton said, rather disagreeably for him. He was most pleasant usually.

"I have simply indicated a possibility," Tish said. "Aggie, I think I'll have a small quantity of blackberry cordial."

With Tish recourse to that remedy indicated either fatigue or a certain nervous strain. That it was the latter was shown by the fact that when Mr. Burton had gone she started the engine of the car and suggested that we be ready to leave at a moment's notice. She then took a folding chair and placed herself in a dark corner of the ruined house.

"If you see the lights of a car approaching," she called, "just tell me, will you?"

However, I am happy to say that no car came near. Somewhat later Mr. Burton appeared rolling a tire ahead of him, and wearing the dazed look he still occasionally wore when confronted with new evidences of Tish's efficiency.

"Well," he said, dropping the tire and staring at Aggie and myself, "she dreamed true. Either that or —"

"Mr. Burton," Tish called, "do you mind hiding that tire until morning? We found it and it is ours. But it's unnecessary to excite suspicion at any time."

I am not certain that Mr. Burton's theory is right, but even if it is I contend that war is war and justifies certain practices hardly to be condoned in times of peace.

Briefly, he has always maintained that Tish being desperate and arguing that the C. in C. — which is military for commander-in-chief — was able to secure tires whenever necessary — that Tish had deliberately unfastened a spare tire from the rear of General Pershing's automobile; not of course actually salvaging it, but leaving it in a position where on the car's getting into motion it would fall off and could then be salvaged.

I do not know. I do know, however, that Tish retired very early to her bed in the ambulance. As Aggie was heating water for a bath, having found a sheltered horse trough behind a broken wall, I took Mr. Burton for a walk through the town in an endeavor to bring him to a more cheerful frame of mind. He was still very low-spirited, but he offered no confidences until we approached the only undestroyed building in sight. He stopped then and suggested turning back.

"It's a Y hut," he said. "We'll be about as welcome there as a skunk at a garden party."

I reprimanded him for this, as I had found no evidence of any jealousy between the two great welfare organizations. But when I persisted in advancing he said: "Well, you might as well know it. She's there. I saw her through a window."

"What has that got to do with my getting a bottle of vanilla extract there if they have one?"

"Oh, she'll have one probably; she uses it for fudge! I'm not going there, and that's flat."

"I thought you had forgotten her."

"I have!" he said savagely. "The way you forget the toothache. But I don't go round boring a hole in a tooth to get it again. Look here, Miss Lizzie, do you know what she was doing when I saw her? She was dropping six lumps of sugar into a cup of something for that — that parent she's gone bugs about."

"That's what she's here for."

"Oh, it is, is it?" he snarled. "Well, she wasn't doing it for the fellow with a cauliflower ear who was standing beside him. There was a line of about twenty fellows there putting in their own sugar, all right."

"I'll tell you this, Mr. Burton," I said in a serious tone, "sometimes I think things are just as well as they are. You haven't a disposition for marriage. I don't believe you'll make her happy, even if you do get her."

"Oh, I'll not get her," he retorted roughly. "As a matter of fact, I don't want her. I'm cured. I'm as cured as a ham. She can feed sugar to the whole blamed Army, as far as I'm concerned. And after that she can go home and feed sugar to his five kids, and give 'em colic and sit up at night and —"

I left him still muttering and went into the Y hut. Hilda gave a little scream of joy when she saw me and ran round the counter, which was a plank on two barrels, and kissed me. I must say she was a nice little thing.

"Isn't France small after all?" she demanded. "And do you know I've seen your nephew — or is it Miss Tish's? He's just too dear! We had a long talk here only a day or two ago, and I was telling about you three, and suddenly he said: 'Wait a minute. You've mentioned no names, but I'll bet my tin hat my Aunt Tish was one of them!' Isn't that amazing?"

Well, I thought it was, and I took a cup of her coffee. But it was poor stuff, and right then and there I made a kettleful and showed her how. But I noticed she grew rather quiet after a while.

At last she said: "You — I don't suppose you've seen that Mr. Burton anywhere, have you?"

"We saw something of him in Paris," I replied, and glanced out the window. He was standing across what had once been the street, and if ever I've seen hungry eyes in a human being he had them.

"He was so awfully touchy, Miss Lizzie," she said. "And then I was never sure — Why do you suppose he isn't fighting? Not that it's any affair of mine, but I used to wonder."

"He's got a milk leg," I said, and set the coffee kettle off.

"A milk leg! A milk — Oh, how ridiculous! How — Why, Miss Lizzie, how can he?"

"Don't ask me. They get 'em sometimes too. They're very painful. My cousin, Nancy Lee McMasters, had one after her third child and —"

I am sorry to say that here she began to laugh. She laughed all over the hut, really, and when she had stood up and held to the plank and laughed she sat down on a box of condensed milk and laughed again. I am a truthful woman, and I had thought it was time she knew the facts, but I saw at once that I had make a mistake. And when I looked out the window Mr. Burton had gone.

I remained there with her for some time, but as any mention of Mr. Burton only started her off again we discussed other matters.

She said Charlie Sands was in the Intelligence Department at the Front, and that when he left he was about to, as she termed it, pull off a raid.

"He's gone to bring me a German as a souvenir; and that Captain Weber — you remember him — he is going to bring me another," she cried. "He gave me my choice and I took an officer, with a nice upcurled mustache and —"

"And five children?"

"Five children? Whatever do you mean, Miss Lizzie?"

"I understand that Captain Weber has five. I didn't know but that you had a special preference for them that way."

"Why, Miss Lizzie!" she said in a strained voice. "I don't believe it. He's never said —"

I was washing out her dish towels by that time, for she wasn't much of a housekeeper, I'll say that, though as pretty as a picture, and I never looked up. She walked round the hut, humming to herself to show how calm she was, but I noticed that when her broom fell over she kicked at it.

Finally she said: "I don't know why you think I was interested in Captain Weber. He was amusing, that's all; and I like fighting men — the bravest are the tenderest, you know. I — if you ever happen on Mr. Burton you might tell him I'm here. It's interesting, but I get lonely sometimes. I don't see a soul I really care to talk to."

Well, I promised I would, and as Mr. Burton had gone I went back alone. Tish was asleep with a hot stone under her cheek, from which I judged she'd had neuralgia, and Aggie was nowhere in sight. But round the corner an ammunition train of trucks had come in and I suddenly remembered Aggie and her horse trough. Unfortunately I had not asked her where it was.

I roused Tish but her neuralgia had ruffled her usual placid temper, and she said that if Aggie was caught in a horse trough let her sit in it. If she could take a bath in a pint of water Aggie could, instead of hunting up luxuries. She then went to sleep again, leaving me in an anxious frame of mind.

Mr. Burton was not round, and at last I started out alone with a flashlight, but as we were short of batteries I was too sparing of it and stepped down accidentally into a six-foot cellar, jarring my spine badly. When I got out at last it was very late, and though there were soldiers all round I did not like to ask them to assist me in my search, as I had every reason to believe that our dear Aggie had sought cleanliness in her nightgown.

It was, I believe, fully 2 A. M. when I finally discovered her behind a wall, where a number of our boys were playing a game with a lantern and dice — a game which consisted apparently of coaxing the inanimate objects with all sorts of endearing terms. They got up when they saw me, but I observed that I was merely taking a walk, and wandered as nonchalantly as I was able into the inclosure.

At first all was dark and silent. Then I heard the trickle of running water, and a moment later a sneeze. The lost was found!

"Aggie!" I said sternly.

"Hush, for Heaven's sake! They'll hear you."

"Where are you?"

"B-b-behind the trough," she said, her teeth chattering. "Run and get my bathrobe, Lizzie. Those d-d-dratted boys have been there for an hour."

Well, I had brought it with me, and she had her slippers; and we started back. I must say that Aggie was a strange figure, however, and one of the boys said after we had passed: "Well, fellows, war's hell, all right."

"If you saw it too I feel better," said another. "I thought maybe this frog liquor was doing things to me."

Aggie, however, was sneezing and did not hear.

I come now to that part of my narrative which relates to Charlie Sands' raid and the results which followed it. I felt a certain anxiety about telling Tish of the dangerous work in which he was engaged, and waited until her morning tea had fortified her. She was, I remember, sitting on a rock directing Mr. Burton, who was changing a tire.

"A raid?" she said. "What sort of a raid?"

"To capture Germans, Tish."

"A lot of chance he'll have!" she said with a sniff. "What does he know about raids? And you'd think to hear you talk, Lizzie, that pulling Germans out of a trench was as easy as letting a dog out after a neighbor's cat. It's like Pershing and all the rest of them," she added bitterly, "to take a left-handed newspaper man, who can't shut his right eye to shoot with the left, and start him off alone to take the whole German Army."

"He wouldn't go alone," said Mr. Burton.

"Certainly not!" Tish retorted. "I know him, and you don't, Mr. Burton. He'll not go alone. Of course not! He'll pick out a lot of men who play good bridge, or went to college with him, or belong to his fraternity, or can sing, or some such reason, and —"

Here to my great surprise she flung down one of our two last remaining teacups and retired precipitately into the ruins. Not for us to witness her majestic grief. Rachel — or was it Naomi? — mourning for her children.

However, in a short time she reappeared and stated that she was sick of fooling round on back roads, and that we would now go directly to the Front.

"We'll never pull it off," Mr. Burton said to me in an undertone.

"She has never failed, Mr. Burton," I reminded him gravely.

Before we started Mr. Burton saw Hilda, but he came back looking morose and savage. He came directly to me.

"Look me over," he said. "Do I look queer or anything?"

"Not at all," I replied.

"Look again. I don't seem to be dying on my feet, do I? Anything wan about me? I don't totter with feebleness, do I?"

"You look as strong as a horse," I said somewhat acidly.

"Then I wish to thunder you'd tell me," he stormed, "why that girl — that — well, you know who I mean — why the deuce she should first giggle all over the place when she sees me, and then baby me like an idiot child? 'Here's a chair,' she'd say, and 'Do be careful of yourself'; and when I recovered from that enough to stand up like a man and ask for a cup of coffee she said I ought to take soup; it was strengthening!"

Fortunately Tish gave the signal to start just then, and we moved out. Hilda was standing in her doorway when we passed, and I thought she looked rather forlorn. She blew kisses to us, but Mr. Burton only saluted stiffly and looked away. I have often considered that to the uninitiated the ways of love are very strange.

It was when we were out of the village that he turned to me with a strange look in his eyes.

"She doesn't care for Weber after all," he said. "Didn't I tell you the minute she found she could have him she wouldn't want him? Do you think I'd marry a girl like that?"

"She's a nice little thing," I replied. "But you're perfectly right — she's no housekeeper."

"No housekeeper!" he said in a tone of astonishment. "That's the cleanest hut in France. And let me tell you I've had the only cup of coffee —"

He broke off and fell into a fit of abstraction. Somewhat later he looked up and said: "I'll never see her again, Miss Lizzie."

"Why?"

"Because I told her I wouldn't come back until I could bring her a German officer as a souvenir. Some idiot had told her he was going to, and, of course, I told her if she was collecting them I'd get her one. A fat chance I have too! I don't know what made me do it. I'm only surprised I didn't make it the Crown Prince while I was at it."

But how soon were our thoughts to turn from soft thoughts of love to graver matters!

Tish, as I have said before, has a strange gift of foresight that amounts almost to prophecy.

I have never known her, for instance, to put a pink bow on an afghan and then have the subsequent development turn out to be a boy, or vice versa. And the very day before Mr. Ostermaier fell and sprained his ankle she had picked up a roller chair at an auction sale, and in twenty minutes he was in it.

At noon we stopped at a crossroads and distributed to some passing troops our usual cigarettes and chocolate. We also fried a number of doughnuts, and were given three cheers by various companies as they passed. It was when our labors were over that Tish perceived a broken machine gun abandoned by the roadside, and spent some time examining it.

"One never knows," she said, "what bits of knowledge may one day be useful."

Mr. Burton explained the mechanism to her.

"I'd be firing one of these things now," he said gloomily, "if it were not for that devilish piece of American ingenuity, the shower bath."

"Good gracious!" Aggie said.

"Fact. I got into a machine-gun school, but one day in a shower one of the officers perceived my — er — affliction, badly swollen from a hike, and reported me."

Tish was strongly inclined to tow the machine gun behind us and eventually have it repaired, but Mr. Burton said it was not worth the trouble, and shortly afterward we turned off the main road into a lane, seeking a place for our luncheon. Tish drove as usual, but she continued to lament the gun.

"I feel keenly," she said, "the necessity of being fully armed against any emergency. And I feel, too, that it is my solemn duty to salvage such weapons as come my way at any and all times."

I called to her just then, but she was driving while looking over her shoulder at Mr. Burton, and it was too late to avoid the goat. We went over it and it lay behind us in the road quite still.

"You've killed it, Tish," I said.

"Not at all," she retorted. "It has probably only fainted. As I was saying, I feel that with our near approach to the lines we should be armed to the teeth with modern engines of destruction, and should also know how to use them."

We were then in a very attractive valley, and Tish descending observed that if it were not for the noise of falling shells and so on it would have been a charming place to picnic.

She then instructed Aggie and me to prepare a luncheon of beef croquettes and floating island, and asked Mr. Burton to accompany her back to the car.

As I was sitting on the running board beating eggs for a meringue at the time I could not avoid overhearing the conversation.

First Mr. Burton, acting under orders, lifted the false bottom, and then he whistled and observed: "Great Cæsar's ghost! Looks as though there is going to be hell up Sixth Street, doesn't it?"

"I'll ask you not to be vulgar, Mr. Burton."

"But — look here, Miss Tish. We'll be jailed for this, you know. You may be able to get away with the C. in C.'s tires, but you can't steal a hundred or so grenades without somebody missing them. Besides, what the — what the dickens are you going to do with them? If it had been eggs now, or oranges — but grenades!"

"They may be useful," Tish replied in her cryptic manner. "Forearmed is forewarned, Mr. Burton. What is this white pin for?"

I believe she then pulled the pin, for I heard Mr. Burton yell, and a second later there was a loud explosion.

I sat still, unable to move, and then I heard Mr. Burton say in a furious voice: "If I hadn't grabbed that thing and thrown it you'd have been explaining this salvage system of yours to your Maker before this, Miss Carberry. Upon my word, if I hadn't known you'd blow up the whole outfit the moment I was gone I'd have left before this. I've got nerves if you haven't."

"That was an over-arm pitch you gave it," was Tish's sole reply. "I had always understood that grenades were thrown in a different manner."

I distinctly heard his groan.

"You'll have about as much use for grenades as I have for pink eye," he said almost savagely. "I don't like to criticize, Miss Tish, and I must say I think to this point we've made good. But when I see you stocking up with grenades instead of cigarettes, and giving every indication of being headed for the Rhine, I feel that it is time to ask what next?"

"Have you any complaint about the last few weeks?" Tish inquired coldly.

"Well, if we continue to leave a trail of depredations behind us — It's bad enough to have a certain person think I'm a slacker, but if she gets the idea that I'm a first-class second-story worker I'm done, that's all."

Fortunately Aggie announced luncheon just then.

Every incident of that luncheon is fixed clearly in my mind, because of what came after it. We had indeed penetrated close to the Front, as was shown by the number of shells which fell in it while we ate. The dirt from one, in fact, quite spoiled the floating island, and we were compelled to open a can of peaches to replace it. It was while we were drinking our after-dinner coffee that Tish voiced the philosophy which upheld her.

"When my hour comes it will come," she said calmly. "Viewed from that standpoint the attempts of the enemy to disturb us become amusing — nothing more."

"Exactly," said Mr. Burton, skimming some dust from the last explosion out of his coffee cup. "Amusing is the word. Funny, I call it. Funny as a crutch. Why, look who's here!"

There was a young officer riding up the valley rapidly. I remember Tish taking a look at him and then saying quickly: "Lizzie, go and close the floor of the ambulance. Don't run. I'll explain later."

Well, the officer rode up and jumped off his horse and saluted.

"Some of our fellows said you were trapped here, Miss Carberry," he said. "I didn't believe it at first. It's a bad place. We'll have to get you out somehow."

"I'm not anxious to get out."

"But," he said, and stared at all of us — "you are — Do you know that our trenches are just beyond this hill?"

"I wish you'd tell the Germans that; they seem to think they are in this valley."

He laughed a little and said: "They ought to make you a general, Miss Carberry." He then said to Mr. Burton: "I'd like to speak to you for a moment."

Looking back I believe that Tish had a premonition of trouble then, for during their conversation aside she got out her knitting, always with her an indication of perturbation or of deep thought, and she spoke rather sharply to Aggie about rinsing the luncheon dishes more thoroughly. Aggie said afterward that she herself had felt at that time that peculiar itching in the palms of her hands which always with her presages bad news.

"If he asks about those grenades, Lizzie, you can reply. Say you don't know anything about them. That's the truth."

"I know where they are," I said with some acidity. "And what's more, I know I'm not going to ride a foot in that ambulance with that concentrated extract of hell under my feet."

"Lizzie —"

She began sternly, but just then the two men came back, and the officer's face was uncomfortable.

"I — from your demeanor," he said, "and — er — the fact that you haven't mentioned it I rather gather that you have not heard the er — the news, Miss Carberry."

"I didn't see the morning papers," Tish said with the dry wit so characteristic of her.

"You have a nephew, I understand, at the Front?"

Tish's face suddenly grew set and stern.

"Have — or had?" she asked in a terrible voice.

"Oh, it's not so bad as all that. In fact, he's a lot safer just now than you are, for instance. But it's rather unfortunate in a way too. He has been captured by the enemy."

Aggie ran to her then with the blackberry cordial, but Tish waved her away.

"A prisoner!" she said. "A nephew of mine has allowed himself to be captured by the Germans? It is incredible!"

"Lots of us are doing it," he said. "It's no disgrace. In fact, it's a mark of courage. A fellow goes farther than he ought to, and the first thing he knows he's got a belt of bayonet points, and it is a time for discretion."

"Leave me, please," Tish said majestically. "I am ashamed. I am humbled. I must think."

Shortly after that she called us back and said: "I have come to this conclusion: The situation is unbearable and must be rectified. Do you know where he is enduring this shameful captivity?"

"I wouldn't take it too hard, Miss Tish," said the officer. "He's very comfortable, as we happen to know. One of our runners got back at dawn this morning. He said he left your nephew in the church at V — , playing pinochle with the German C. O. The runner was hidden in the cellar under the church, and he said the C. O. had lost all his money and his Iron Cross, and was going to hold Captain Sands until he could win them back."

He then urged her, the moment night fell, to retire from our dangerous position, and to feel no anxiety whatever.

"If I know him," were his parting words, "he'll pick that German as clean as a chicken. Pinochle will win the war," he added and rode away.

During the remainder of the afternoon Tish sat by herself, knitting and thinking. It was undoubtedly then that she formed the plan which in its execution has brought us so much hateful publicity, yet without which the town of V — might still be in German hands.

II

We knew, of course, that Tish's fine brain was working on the problem of rescuing Charlie Sands; and Mr. Burton was on the whole rather keen about it.

"I've got to get a German officer some way," he said. "She's probably planning now to see Von Hindenburg about Sands. She generally aims high, I've discovered. And in that case I rather fancy myself taking the old chap back to Hilda as a souvenir." He then reflected and scowled. "But she'd be flirting with him in ten minutes, damn her!" he added.

Tish refused both sympathy and conversation during the afternoon.

On Aggie's offering her both she merely said: "Go away and leave me alone, for Heaven's sake. He is perfectly safe. I only hope he took his toothbrush, that's all."

It is a proof of Tish's gift of concentration that she thought out her plan so thoroughly under the circumstances, for the valley was shelled all that afternoon. We found an abandoned battery position and the three of us took refuge in it, leaving Tish outside knitting calmly. It was a poor place, but by taking in our folding table and chairs we made it fairly comfortable, and Mr. Burton taught us a most interesting game of cards, in which one formed pairs and various combinations, and counted with coffee beans. If one had four of any one kind one took all the beans.

It was dusk when Tish appeared in the doorway, and we noticed that she wore a look of grim determination.

"I have been to the top of the hill," she said, "and I believe that I know now the terrain thoroughly. In case my first plan fails we may be compelled to desperate measures — but I find my present situation intolerable. Never before has a member of my family been taken by an enemy. We die, but we do not surrender."

"You can speak for your own family, then," Aggie said. "I've got a family, too, but it's got sense enough to surrender when necessary. And if you think Libby Prison was any treat to my grandfather —"

Tish ignored her.

"It is my intention," she went on, "to appeal to the general of his division to rescue my nephew and thus wipe out the stain on the family honor. Failing that, I am prepared to go to any length." Here she eyed Aggie coldly. "It is no time for craven spirits," she said. "We may be arrested and court-martialed for being so near the Front, to say nothing of what may eventuate in case of a refusal. I intend to leave no stone unturned, but I think it only fair to ask for a vote of confidence. Those in the affirmative will please signify by saying 'aye.'"

"Aye," I said stoutly. I would not fail my dear Tish in such a crisis. Aggie followed me a moment later, but feebly, and Mr. Burton said: "I don't like the idea any more than I do my right eye. Why bother with the general? I'm for going to V — and breaking up the pinochle game, and bringing home the bacon in the shape of a Hun or two."

However, I have reason to think that he was joking, and that subsequent events startled him considerably, for I remember that when it was all over and we were in safety once again he kept saying over and over in a dazed voice: "Well, can you beat it? Can you beat it?"

In some way Tish had heard, from a battery on the hill, I think, that headquarters was at the foot of the hill on the other side. She made her plans accordingly.

"As soon as darkness has fallen," she said to Mr. Burton, "we three women shall visit the commanding officer and there make our plea — without you, as it will be necessary to use all the softening feminine influence possible. One of two things will then occur: Either he will rescue my nephew or — I shall."

"Now see here, Miss Tish," he protested, "you're not going to leave me out of it altogether, are you? You wouldn't break my heart, would you? Besides, you'll need me. I'm a specialist at rescuing nephews. I — I've rescued thousands of nephews in my time."

Well, she'd marked out a place that would have been a crossroads if the German shells had left any road, and she said if she failed with the C. O. he was to meet us there, with two baskets of cigarettes for the men in the trenches.

"Cigarettes!" he said. "What help will they be against the enemy? Unless you mean to wait until they've smoked themselves to death."

"Underneath the cigarettes," Tish went on calmly, "you will have a number of grenades. If only we could repair that machine gun!" she reflected. "I dare say I can salvage an automatic rifle or two," she finished; "though large-sized firecrackers would do. The real thing is to make a noise."

"We might get some paper bags and burst them," suggested Mr. Burton; "and if you feel that music would add to the martial effect I can play fairly well on a comb."

It was perhaps nine o'clock when we reached the crest of the hill, and had Tish not thoughtfully brought her wire cutters along I do not believe we would have succeeded in reaching headquar-

ters. We got there finally, however, and it was in a cellar and —
though I do not care to reflect on our gallant army — not as tidy as
it should have been. Mr. Burton having remained behind temporarily the three of us made our way to the entrance, and Tish was
almost bayoneted by a sentry there, who was nervous because of a
number of shells falling in the vicinity.

"Take that thing away!" she said with superb scorn, pointing
to the bayonet. "I don't want a hole in the only uniform I've got,
young man. Watch your head, Lizzie!"

"The saints protect us!" said the sentry. "Women! Three
women!"

Tish and I went down the muddy incline into the cellar, and
two officers who were sitting there playing cribbage looked at us
and then stood up with a surprised expression.

Tish had assumed a most lofty attitude, and picking out the
general with an unfailing eye she saluted and said: "Only the most
urgent matters would excuse my intrusion, sir. I —"

Unfortunately at that moment Aggie slipped and slid into the
room feet first in a sitting posture. She brought up rather dazed
against the table, and for a moment both officers were too surprised to offer her any assistance. Tish and I picked her up, and
she fell to sneezing violently, so that it was some time before the
conversation was resumed. It was the general who resumed it.

"This is very flattering," he said in a cold voice, "but if you
ladies will explain how you got here I'll make it interesting for
somebody."

Suddenly the colonel who was with him said: "Suffering
Crimus! It can't be! And yet — it certainly is!"

We looked at him, and it was the colonel who had been so
interested in Charlie Sands at the training camp. We all shook
hands with him, and he offered us chairs, and said to the general:
"These are the ladies I have told you about, sir, with the nephew.
You may recall the helpful suggestions sent to the Secretary of War
and forwarded back to me by the General Staff. I have always
wanted to explain about those dish towels, ladies. You see, you
happened on us at a bad time. Our dish towels had come, but
though neatly hemmed they lacked the small tape in the corner by
which to hang them up. I therefore —"

"Oh, keep still!" said the general in an angry tone. "Now, what
brings you women here?"

"My nephew has been taken prisoner," Tish said coldly. "I
want to know merely whether you propose to do anything about it
or intend to sit here in comfort and do nothing."

He became quite red in the face at this allusion to the cribbage board, et cetera, and at first seemed unable to speak.

"Quietly, man," said the colonel. "Remember your blood pressure."

"Damn my blood pressure!" said the general in a thick tone.

I must refuse to relate the conversation that followed — hardly conversation, indeed, as at the end the general did all the talking.

At last, however, he paused for breath, and Tish said very quietly: "Then I am to understand that you refuse to do anything about my nephew?"

"Who is your nephew?"

"Charlie Sands."

"And who's Charlie Sands?"

"My nephew," said Tish.

He said nothing to this, but shouted abruptly in a loud voice: "Orderly! Raise that curtain and let some air into this rat hole."

Then he turned to the colonel and said: "Thompson, you're younger than I am. I've got a family, and my blood pressure's high. I'm going out to make a tour of the observation posts."

"Coward!" said the colonel to him in a low tone.

The colonel was very pleasant to us when the other man had gone. The general was his brother-in-law, he said, and rather nervous because they hadn't had a decent meal for a week.

"The only thing that settles his nerves is cribbage," he explained. "It helps his morale. Now — let us think about getting you back to safety. I'd offer you our humble hospitality, but somebody got in here today and stole the duckboard I've been sleeping on, and I can't offer you the general's cellar door. He's devoted to it."

"What if we refuse to go back?" Tish demanded. "We've taken a risky trip for a purpose, and I don't give up easily, young man. I'm inclined to sit here until that general promises to do something."

His face changed.

"Oh, now see here," he said in an appealing voice, "you aren't going to make things difficult for me, are you? There's a regulation against this sort of thing."

"We are welfare workers," Tish said calmly. "Behind us there stand the entire American people. If kept from the front trenches while trying to serve our boys there are ways of informing the people through the press."

"It's exactly the press I fear," he said in a sad voice. "Think of the results to you three, and to me."

"What results?" Tish demanded impatiently. "I'm not doing anything I'm ashamed of."

He was abstractedly moving the cribbage pins about.

"It's like this," he said: "Not very far behind the lines there are a lot of newspaper correspondents, and lately there hasn't been much news. But perhaps I'd better explain my own position. I am engaged to a lovely girl at home. I write to her every day, but I have been conscious recently that in her replies to me there has been an element of — shall I say suspicion? No, that is not the word. Anxiety — of anxiety, lest I shall fall in love with some charming Red Cross or Y. M. C. A. girl. Nothing could be further from my thoughts, but you can see my situation. Three feminine visitors at nightfall; news-hungry correspondents; all the rest of it. Scandal, dear ladies! And absolute ruin to my hopes!"

"Bosh!" said Tish. But I could see that she was uncomfortable. "If there's trouble I'll send her our birth certificates. Besides, I thought you said the general was your brother-in-law?"

Aggie says he changed color at that but he said hastily: "By marriage, madam, only by marriage. By that I mean — I — he — the general is married to my brother."

"Really!" said Tish. "How unusual!"

She said afterward that she saw at once then that we were only wasting time, and that neither one of them would move hand or foot to get Charlie Sands back. Aggie had been scraping her skirt with a table knife, and was now fairly tidy, so Tish prepared to depart.

"On thinking it over," she said, "I realize that I am confronting a situation which requires brains rather than brute force. I shall therefore attend to it myself. Good night, colonel. I hope you find another duckboard. And — if you are writing home present my compliments to the general's husband. Come, Aggie."

At the top of the incline I looked back. The colonel was staring after us and wiping his forehead with a khaki handkerchief.

"You see," Tish said bitterly, "that is the sort of help one gets from the Army." She drew a deep breath and looked in the general direction of the trenches. "One thing is sure and certain — I'm not going back until I've found out whether Charlie Sands is still in that town over there or whether he has been taken away so we'll have to get at him from Switzerland."

Aggie gave a low moan at this, and Tish eyed her witheringly.

"Don't be an idiot, Aggie!" she observed. "I haven't asked you to go — or Lizzie either. I'd be likely," she added, "to get through

our lines unseen and into the very midst of the German Army —
with one of you sneezing with hay fever and the other one panting
like a locomotive from, too much flesh."

"Tish — " I began firmly. But she waved her hand in silence
and demanded Aggie's flashlight. She then led the way behind the
ruins of a wall and took a bundle of papers from under her jacket.

"If the Army won't help us we have a right to help ourselves,"
she observed. And I perceived with a certain trepidation that the
papers were some that had been lying on the table at headquarters.

"'Memorandum,'" Tish read the top one. "'Write home.
Order boots. Send to British Commissary for Scotch whisky.
Insect powder!' Wouldn't you know," she said bitterly, "that that
general would have to make a memorandum about writing
home?"

Underneath, however, there was an aeroplane picture of the
Front and V — , and also a map. Both of these she studied carefully until several bullets found their way to our vicinity, and a
sentry ran up and was very rude about the light. On receiving a
box of cigarettes, however, he became quite friendly.

"Haven't had a pill for a week," he said. "Got to a point now
where we steal the hay from the battery horses and roll it up in
leaves from my Bible. But it isn't really satisfying."

Tish gave him a brief lecture on thus mutilating his best
friend, but he said that he only used the unimportant pages. "You
know," he explained — "somebody begat somebody else, and that
sort of thing. You haven't any more fags about you, have you?" he
asked wistfully. "I'll be sandbagged and robbed if I go back
without any for the other fellows."

"We can bring some," Tish suggested, "and you might show us
to the trenches. I particularly wish to give some to the men in the
most advanced positions."

"You're on," he said cheerfully. "Bring the life savers, and
we'll see that you get forward all right."

Tish reflected.

"Suppose," she said at last — "suppose that we wish to be able
on returning to our native land to state that we have not only been
to our advanced positions but have even made a short excursion
into the debatable territory — that is, into what is commonly
known as No Man's Land?"

"All of you?" he asked doubtfully.

"All of us."

He then considered and said: "How many cigarettes have you

got?"

"About a hundred packages," Tish replied. "Say, five to you, and the rest used where considered most efficacious."

"Every man has his price," he observed. "That's mine. I'm taking a chance, but I've seen you round, so I know you're not spies. And if you get an extra helmet out there you might give me one. I've been here six months and I've never seen one, on a German or off. I let a woman reporter through last week," he added, "and d'you think she thanked me? No. She gave me hell because the Germans had a raid that night and nearly got her. I'm a soldier, not a prophet."

Tish left us immediately to go back to Mr. Burton, and Aggie clutched at my arm in a frenzy of anxiety.

"She's going to do it, Lizzie!" she said with her teeth chattering. "She's going to V — to rescue Charlie Sands, and we'll all be caught, and — Lizzie, I feel that I shall never see home again."

"Well, if you ask me, I don't think you will," I said as calmly as possible. Aggie put her head on my shoulder and wept between sneezes.

"I know I'm weak, Lizzie," she moaned, "but I'm frightened, and I'm not afraid to say so. You'd think she only had to shoo those Germans like a lot of chickens. I love Tish, but if she'd only sprain her ankle or something!"

However, Tish came back soon, bringing Mr. Burton with her and two baskets with cigarettes on top and grenades below, and also our revolvers and a supply of extra cartridges. She had not explained her plan to Mr. Burton, so we sat down behind the wall and she told him. He seemed quite willing and cheerful.

"Certainly," he said. "It is all quite clear. We simply go into No Man's Land for souvenirs, and they pass us. Perfectly natural, of course. We then continue to advance to the German lines, and then commit suicide. I've been thinking of doing it for some time anyhow, and this way has an element of the dramatic that appeals to me." I have learned since that he felt that the only thing to do was to humor Tish, and that he was convinced that about a hundred yards in No Man's Land would hurt no one, and, as he expressed it, clear the air. How little he knew our dear Tish!

As it is not my intention to implicate any of those brave boys who sought to give us merely the innocent pleasure of visiting the strip of land between the two armies I shall draw a veil over our excursion through the trenches that night, where we were met everywhere with acclaim and gratitude, and finally assisted out of the trenches by means of a ladder. As it was quite dark the grenades in the basket entirely escaped notice, and we found ourselves at last headed toward the German lines, and fully armed, though looking, as Mr. Burton observed, like a picnic party.

He persisted in making humorous sallies such as: "Did any one remember the pepper and salt?" and "I hope somebody brought pickles. What's a picnic without pickles?"

I regret to say that we were fired on by some of our own soldiers who didn't understand the situation, shortly after this, and that the bottle of blackberry cordial which I was carrying was broken to fragments.

"If they hit this market basket there'll be a little excitement," Mr. Burton said. He then stopped and said that a joke was a joke, but there was such a thing as carrying it too far, and that we'd better look for a helmet or two and then go back.

"The Germans are just on the other side of that wood," he whispered; "and they don't know a joke when they see one."

"I thought, Mr. Burton, you promised to take Hilda a German officer," Tish said scornfully.

"I did," he agreed. "I did indeed. But now I think of it, I didn't promise her a live one. The more I consider the matter the more I am sure that no stipulation was made as to the conditions of delivery. I —"

But when he saw Tish continuing to advance he became very serious, and even suggested that if we would only go back he would himself advance as far as possible and endeavor to reach V —.

Just what Tish's reply would have been I do not know, as at that moment Aggie stumbled and fell into a deep shell hole full of water. We heard the splash and waited for her voice, as we were uncertain of her exact position.

But what was our surprise on hearing a deep masculine voice say: "Hands up, you dirty swine!"

"Let go of me," came in piteous accents from Aggie.

There was then complete silence, until the other voice said: "Well, I'll be damned!" It then said: "Bill, Bill!"

"Here," said still another voice, a short distance away, in a sort of loud whisper.

"There's a mermaid in my pool," said the first voice. "Did you draw anything?"

"Lucky devil," said the other voice. "I'm drawing about eight feet of water, that's all."

Tish then advanced in the direction of the voices and said: "Aggie, are you all right?"

"I'm half drowned. And there's a man here."

The first voice then said in an aggrieved manner: "This is my puddle, you know, lady. And if my revolver wasn't wet through I'm afraid there would be one mermaid less, or whatever you are."

The Germans at that moment sent up one of their white lights, which resemble certain of our Fourth of July pieces, which float a long time and give the effect of full moonlight.

"Down," said Mr. Burton, and we all fell flat on our faces. Before doing so, however, we had a short glimpse of Aggie's head and another above the water in the shell hole, and realized that her position was very uncomfortable.

When the light died away the two men emerged, and with some difficulty dragged her out. It was while this was going on that Tish caught my arm and whispered: "Lizzie, I have heard that voice before."

Well, it had a familiar sound to me also, and when he addressed the other man as Grogan I suddenly remembered. It was the man we had thrown from the ambulance in Paris the night Tish salvaged it! I told Tish in a whisper, and she remembered the incident clearly.

"You sure gave me a scare," he said to Aggie. "For if you were a German I was gone, and if you were an officer of the A. E. F. I was gone more. Bill and I just slipped out to take a look round the town behind those woods, account of our captain being a prisoner there."

"Who is your captain?" Tish asked.

"Name's Weber. We pulled off a raid last night, and he and a fellow named Sands got grabbed."

"Weber?" said Mr. Burton, forgetting to whisper.

"You — you don't mean Captain Weber?" I asked after a sickening pause.

"That's the man."

"Oh, dear!" said Aggie.

Suddenly Mr. Burton stopped and put down the basket of grenades.

"I'm damned if I'm going to rescue him!" he said firmly. "Now look here, Miss Tish, I hate to disappoint you, but I've got private reasons for leaving Weber exactly where he is.

"I don't wish him any harm, but if they'd take him and put him to road mending for three or four years I'd be a happier man. And as far as I'm concerned, I'm going to give them the chance."

The two men had stood listening, and now Bill spoke:

"Am I to understand that this is a rescue party?" he said.

"Seeing the basket I thought it was a picnic. I just want to say this: If you have any idea of going to V — , and as we were going in that direction ourselves, we might combine. My friend here and I were over last night, and we know how to get into the town."

"Very well," Tish agreed after a moment's hesitation. "I have no objection. It must be distinctly understood, however, that I am in charge. Captain Sands is my nephew."

Another light went up just then, and I perceived that he was staring at her.

"My — my word!" he gasped.

We then fell on our faces, and while lying there I heard him whispering to Bill. He then said to Tish: "I believe, lady, that we have met before."

"Very possibly," Tish said calmly. "In the course of my welfare work I have met many of our brave men."

"I wouldn't call it exactly welfare work you were doing when I saw you."

"No?" said Tish.

"You may be interested to know that if you hadn't stolen that ambulance —"

"Salvaged."

" — salvaged that ambulance I would now be in safety in Paris, instead of — Not that I'd exchange," he added. "I wouldn't have missed this excursion for a good bit. But they made it so darned unpleasant for me that I enlisted."

The starlight having now died we rose and prepared to advance. Mr. Burton, however, was very difficult and tried to get Tish to promise to leave Captain Weber if we found him.

"It's the only bit of luck I've had since I left home, Miss Tish," he said.

Tish, however, ignored him, and with the help of our new allies briefly sketched a plan of campaign.

I make no pretensions to military knowledge, but I shall try to explain the situation at V — , as our dear Tish learned it from the general's papers and the two soldiers. The real German position — a military term meaning location and not attitude — was behind the town, but they kept enough soldiers in it to hold it, and in case of an attack they filled it up with great rapidity. So far the church tower remained standing, as the Allies wished on taking the town to use it to look out from and observe any unfriendly actions on the part of the Germans.

"If only," Tish said, "we could have repaired that machine gun and brought it the affair would be extremely simple. It has from the beginning been my intention to give the impression of an attack in force."

She then considered for a short time, and finally suggested that the two soldiers return to the allied Front and attempt to secure two automatic rifles.

"And it might be as well," she added, "to take Miss Aggie with you. She is wet through, and will undoubtedly before long have a return of her hay fever, which with her has no season. A sneeze at a critical time might easily ruin us."

Aggie, however, absolutely refused to return, and said that by holding her nostrils closed and her mouth open she could, if she felt the paroxysm coming on, sneeze almost noiselessly. She said also that though not related to her by blood Charlie Sands was as dear as her own, and that if turned back she would go to V — alone and, if captured, at least suffer imprisonment with him.

Tish was quite touched, I could see, and on the two men departing to attempt the salvage of the required weapons she assisted me in wringing out Aggie's clothing and in making her as comfortable as possible.

We waited for some time, eating chocolate to restore our strength, and attempting to comfort Mr. Burton, who was very surly.

"It has been my trouble all my life," he observed bitterly, "not to leave well enough alone. I hadn't any hope of the success of this expedition before, but now I know you'll pull it off. You'll get Sands and you'll get Weber and send him back — to — well, you understand. It's just my luck. I'm not complaining, but if I'm killed and he isn't I'm going to haunt that Y hut and make it darned unpleasant for both of them."

Tish reproved him for debasing the future life to such purposes, but he was firm.

"If you think I'm going to stand round and be walked through and sat on, and all the indignities that ghosts must suffer, without getting back," he said gloomily, "you can think again, Miss Tish!"

When the two men returned Tish gave them a brief talking-to.

"First of all," she said, "there must be no mistake as to who is in command of this expedition. If we succeed it will be by finesse rather than force, and that is distinctly a feminine quality. Second, there is to be no unnecessary fighting. We are here to secure my nephew, not the German Army."

The man we had bumped off the step of the ambulance, whose name proved to be Jim, said at once that that last sentence had relieved his mind greatly. A few prisoners wouldn't put them out seriously, but the Allies were feeding more than they could afford already.

"But a few won't matter," he added. "Say, a dozen or so. They won't kick on that."

I have never learned where Tish learned her strategy — unless from the papers she took from the general's cellar.

Military experts have always considered the plan masterly, I believe, and have lauded the mobility of a small force and the greater element of surprise possible, as demonstrated by the incidents which followed.

Briefly Tish adhered to her plan of making the attack seem a large one, by spreading the party over a large area and having it make as much noise as possible.

"By firing from one spot, and then running rapidly either to right or left, and firing again," she said, "those who have only revolvers may easily appear to be several persons instead of one."

She then arranged that the two automatic rifles attack the town from in front, but widely separated, while Aggie and myself, endeavoring to be a platoon — or perhaps she said regiment — would advance from the left. On the right Mr. Burton was to move forward in force, firing his revolver and throwing grenades in different directions. Of her own plans she said nothing.

"Forward, the Suicide Club!" said Mr. Burton with that strange sarcasm which had marked him during the last hour.

I have since reflected that certain kinds of men seem to take love very unpleasantly. Aggie, however, maintains that the deeper the love the greater the misery, and that Mr. Wiggins once sent back a muffler she had made for him on seeing her conversing with the janitor of the church about dust in her pew.

In a short time we had passed through the wood and the remainder of the excursion was very slow, owing to being obliged to crawl on our hands and knees. We could now see the church tower, and Tish gave the signal to separate. The men left us at once, but for a short time Tish was near me, as I could tell by an irritated exclamation from her when she became entangled in the enemy's barbed wire. But soon I realized that she had gone. Looking back I believe it was just before we met the Germans who were out laying wire, but I am not quite certain. There were about ten of the enemy, and they almost stepped on Aggie. She said afterward that she was so alarmed that she sneezed, but that having buried her entire face in a mudhole they did not hear her. We lay quite still for some time, and when they had gone and we could move again Tish had disappeared.

However, we obeyed orders and went on moving steadily to the left, and before long we were able to make out the ruins of V — directly before us. They were apparently empty and silent, and concealing ourselves behind a fallen wall we waited for the automatic rifles to give the signal. Aggie had taken cold from her wetting, and could hardly speak.

"I'b sure they've taked Tish," were her first words.

"Not alive," I said grimly.

"Lizzie! Oh, by dear Tish!"

"If you've got to worry," I said rather tartly, "worry about the Germans. It wouldn't surprise me a particle to see her bring in the lot."

Well, the attack started just then and Aggie and I got our revolvers and began shooting as rapidly as possible, firing from the end of the village, and with Mr. Burton's grenades from one side and our revolvers from the other it made a tremendous noise. Aggie and I did our best, I know, to appear to be a large number, firing and then moving to a new point and firing again. I must say from the way those Germans ran toward their own lines behind the town I was not surprised at the rapidity of the final retreat which ended the war. As Aggie said later, we were not there to kill them unless necessary, but they ran so fast at times it was difficult to avoid hitting them. They fairly ran into the bullets.

In a very short time there was not one in sight, but we kept on firing for a trifle longer, and then made for the church, meeting the two privates on the way. When we arrived Mr. Burton was already there and had unfastened a large bolt on the outside of the door. We crowded in, and somebody closed the door and we had a moment to breathe.

"Well, here we are," said Mr. Burton in a quite cheerful tone. "And not a casualty among us — or the Germans either, I fancy, save those that died of heart disease. Are we all here, by the way?"

He then struck a match, and my heart sank.

"Tish!" I cried. "Tish is not here!"

It was then that a voice from the far end of the church said: "Suffering' snakes! I'm delirious, Weber! I knew that beer would get me. I thought I heard —"

Some one was hammering at the door with a revolver, and we heard Tish's dear voice outside saying: "Keep your hands up! *Lizzie!*"

Mr. Burton opened the door and Tish backed in, followed by a figure that was muttering in German. She had both her revolvers pointed at it, and she said: "Close the door, somebody, and get a light. I think it's a general."

Well, Charlie Sands was coming with a candle stuck in the neck of a bottle, and he seemed extremely surprised. He kept stumbling over things and saying "Wake me, Weber," until he had put a hand on my arm.

"It's real," he said then. "It's a real arm. Therefore it is, it must be. And yet —"

"Stop driveling," Tish said sharply, "and tie up this general or whatever he is. I don't trust him. He's got a mean eye."

It has been the opinion of military experts that the reason the enemy had apparently lost its morale and failed to make a counter-attack at once was the early loss of this officer. In fact, a prisoner taken later I believe told the story that V — had been attacked and captured by an entire division, without artillery preparation, and that he himself had seen the commanding officer killed by a shell. But the truth was that Tish, having fallen into an empty trench a moment or so before I missed her, had after recovering from the shock and surprise followed the trench for some distance, finding that she could advance more rapidly than by crawling on the surface.

She had in this manner happened on a dugout where a German officer was sitting at a table with a lighted candle marking the corners of certain playing cards with the point of a pin. He seemed to be in a very bad humor, and was muttering to himself. She waited in the darkness until he had finished, and had shoved the cards into his pocket. When he had extinguished the candle he started back along the trench toward the village, and Tish merely put her two revolvers to his back and captured him.

I pass over the touching reunion between Tish and her beloved nephew. He seemed profoundly affected, and moving out of the candlelight gave way to emotion that fairly shook him. It was when he returned wiping his eyes that he recognized the German officer. He became exceedingly grave at once.

"I trust you understand," he said to him, "that this — er — surprise party is no reflection on your hospitality. And I am glad to point out also that the pinochle game is not necessarily broken up. It can continue until you are moved back behind the Allied lines. I may not," he added, "be able to offer you a church, because if I do say it you people have been wasteful as to churches. But almost any place in our trenches is entirely safe."

He then looked round the group again and said: "Don't tell me Aunt Aggie has missed this! I couldn't bear it."

"Aggie!" I cried. "Where is Aggie?"

It was then that the painful truth dawned on us. Aggie had not entered the church. She was still outside, perhaps wandering alone among a cruel and relentless foe. It was a terrible moment.

I can still see the white and anxious faces round the candle, and Tish's insistence that a search be organized at once to find her. Mr. Burton went out immediately, and returned soon after to say that she was not in sight, and that the retiring Germans were sending up signal rockets and were probably going to rush the town at once.

We held a short council of war then, but there was nothing to do but to retire, having accomplished our purpose. Even Tish felt this, and said that it was a rule of war that the many should not suffer for the few; also that she didn't propose losing a night's sleep to rescue Charlie Sands and then have him retaken again, as might happen any minute.

We put out the candle and left the church, and not a moment too soon, for a shell dropped through the roof behind us, and more followed it at once. I was very uneasy, especially as I was quite sure that between explosions I could hear Aggie's voice far away calling Tish.

We retired slowly, taking our prisoner with us, and turning round to fire toward the enemy now and then. We also called Aggie by name at intervals, but she did not appear. And when we reached the very edge of the town the Germans were at the opposite end of it, and we were obliged to accelerate our pace until lost in the Stygian darkness of the wood.

It was there that I felt Tish's hand on my arm.

"I'm going back," she said in a low tone. "Driveling idiot that she is, I cannot think of her hiding somewhere and sneezing herself into captivity. I am going back, Lizzie."

"Then I go too," I said firmly. "I guess if she's your responsibility she's mine too."

Well, she didn't want me any more than she wanted the measles, but the time was coming when she could thank her lucky stars I was there. However, she said nothing, but I heard her suggesting that we separate, every man for himself, except the prisoner, and work back, to our own side the best way we could.

With her customary thoughtfulness, however, she held a short conversation with Mr. Burton first. I have not mentioned Captain Weber, I believe, since our first entrance into the church, but he was with us, and I had observed Mr. Burton eying him with unfriendly eyes. Indeed, I am quite convinced that the accident of our leaving the church without the captain, and finding him left behind and bolted in, was no accident at all.

Tish merely told Mr. Burton that the prisoner was his, and that if he chose and could manage to present him to Hilda he might as well do it.

"She's welcome to him," she said.

"He's not my prisoner."

"He is now; I give him to you."

Finding him obdurate, however, she resorted to argument.

"It doesn't invalidate an engagement," she said rather brusquely, "for a man to borrow the money for an engagement ring. If it did there would be fewer engagements. If you want to borrow a German prisoner for the same purpose the principle is the same."

He seemed to be weakening.

"I'd like to do it — if only to see her face," he said slowly. "Not but what it's a risk. He's a good-looking devil."

In the end, however, he agreed, and the last we saw of them he was driving the German ahead, with a grenade in one hand and his revolver in the other, and looking happier than he had looked for days.

Almost immediately after that I felt Tish's hand on my arm. We turned and went back toward V — .

Military experts have been rather puzzled by our statement that the Germans did not reënter V — that night, but remained just outside, and that we reached the church again without so much as a how-do-you-do from any of them. I believe the general impression is that they feared a trap. I think they are rather annoyed to learn that there was a period of several hours during which they might safely have taken the town; in fact, the irritable general who was married to the colonel's brother was most unpleasant about it. When everything was over he came to Paris to see us, and he was most unpleasant.

"If you wanted to take the damned town, why didn't you say so?" he roared. "You came in with a long story about a nephew, but it's my plain conviction, madam, that you were flying for higher game than your nephew from the start."

Tish merely smiled coldly.

"Perhaps," she said in a cryptic manner. "But, of course, in these days of war one must be very careful. It is difficult to tell whom to trust."

As he became very red at that she gently reminded him of his blood pressure, but he only hammered on the table and said:

"Another thing, madam. God knows I don't begrudge you the falderals they've been pinning on you, but it seems to me more than a coincidence that your celebrated strategy followed closely the lines of a memorandum, madam, that was missing from my table after your departure."

"My dear man," Tish replied urbanely, "there is a little military word I must remind you of — salvage. As one of your own staff explained it to me one perceives an object necessary to certain operations. If on saluting that object it fails to return the salute I believe the next step is to capture it. Am I not right?"

But I regret to say that he merely picked up his cap and went out of our sitting room, banging the door behind him.

To return. We reached the church safely, and from that working out in different directions we began our unhappy search. However, as it was still very dark I evidently lost my sense of direction, and while peering into a cellar was suddenly shocked by feeling a revolver thrust against my back.

"You are my prisoner," said a voice. "Move and I'll fire."

It was, however, only Tish. We were both despondent by that time, and agreed to give up the search. As it happened it was well we did so, for we had no more than reached the church and seated ourselves on the doorstep in deep dejection when the enemy rushed the village. I confess that my immediate impulse was flight, but Tish was of more heroic stuff.

"They are coming, Lizzie," she said. "If you wish to fly go now. I shall remain. I have too many tender memories of Aggie to desert her."

She then rose and went without haste into the church, which was sadly changed by shell fire in the last two hours, and I followed her. By the aid of the flashlight, cautiously used, we made our way to a break in the floor and Tish suggested that we retire to the cellar, which we did, descending on piles of rubbish. The noise in the street was terrible by that time, but the cellar was quiet enough, save when now and then a fresh portion of the roof gave way.

I was by this time exceedingly nervous, and Tish gave me a mouthful of cordial. She herself was quite calm.

"We must give them time to quiet down," she said. "They sound quite hysterical, and it would be dangerous to be discovered just now. Perhaps we would better find a sheltered spot and get some sleep. I shall need my wits clear in the morning."

It was fortunate for us that the French use the basements of their churches for burying purposes, for by crawling behind a marble sarcophagus we found a sort of cave made by the debris. Owing to that protection the grenades the enemy threw into the cellar did no harm whatever, save to waken Tish from a sound sleep.

"Drat them anyhow!" she said. "I was just dreaming that Mr. Ostermaier had declined a raise in his salary."

"Tish," I said, "suppose they find Aggie?"

She yawned and turned over.

"Aggie's got more brains than you think she has," was her comment. "She hates dying about as much as most people. My own private opinion is and has been that she went back to our lines hours ago."

"Tish!" I exclaimed. "Then why —"

"I just want to try a little experiment," she said drowsily, and was immediately asleep.

At last I slept myself, and when we wakened it was daylight, and the Germans were in full possession of the town. They inspected the church building overhead, but left it quickly; and Tish drew a keen deduction from that.

"Well, that's something in our favor," she said. "Evidently they're afraid the thing will fall in on them."

At eight o'clock she complained of being hungry, and I felt the need of food myself. With her customary promptness she set out to discover food, leaving me alone, a prey to sad misgivings. In a short time, however, she returned and asked me if I'd seen a piece of wire anywhere.

"I've got considerable barbed wire sticking in me in various places," I said rather tartly, "if that will do."

But she only stood, staring about her in the semidarkness.

"A lath with a nail in the end of it would answer," she observed. "Didn't you step on a nail last night?"

Well, I had, and at last we found it. It was in the end of a plank and seemed to be precisely what she wanted. She took it away with her, and was gone some twenty minutes. At the end of that time she returned carrying carefully a small panful of fried bacon.

"I had to wait," she explained. "He had just put in some fresh slices when I got there."

While we ate she explained.

"There is a small opening to the street," she said, "where there is a machine gun, now covered with debris. Just outside I perceived a soldier cooking his breakfast. Of course there was a chance that he would not look away at the proper moment, but he stood up to fill his pipe. I'd have got his coffee too, but in the fight he kicked it over."

"What fight?" I asked.

"He blamed another soldier for taking the bacon. He was really savage, Lizzie. From the way he acted I gather that they haven't any too much to eat."

Breakfast fortified us both greatly, but it also set me to thinking sadly of Aggie, whose morning meal was a crisp slice of bacon, varied occasionally by an egg. I had not Tish's confidence in her escape. And Tish was restless. She insisted on wandering about the cellar, and near noon I missed her for two hours. When she came back she was covered with plaster dust, but she made no explanation.

"I have been thinking over the situation, Lizzie," she said, "and it divides itself into two parts. We must wait until nightfall and then search again for Aggie, in case my judgment is wrong as to her escape. And then there is a higher law than that of friendship. There is our duty to Aggie, and there is also our duty to the nation."

"Well," I said rather shortly, "I guess we've done our duty. We've taken a prisoner. I owe a duty to my backbone, which is sore from these rocks; and my right leg, which has been tied in a knot with cramp for three hours."

"When," Tish broke in, "is a railroad most safe to travel on? Just after a wreck, certainly. And when, then, is a town easiest to capture? Just after it has been captured. Do you think for one moment that they'll expect another raid tonight?"

"Do you think there will be one?" I asked hopefully.

"I know there will."

She would say nothing further, but departed immediately and was gone most of the afternoon. She came back wearing a strange look of triumph, and asked me if I remembered the code Aggie used, but I had never learned it. She was very impatient.

"It's typical of her," she said, "to disappear just when we need her most. If you knew the code and could get rid of the lookout they keep in the tower, while I —"

She broke off and reflected.

"They've got to change the lookout in the tower," she said. "If the one comes down before the other goes up, and if we had a hatchet —"

"Exactly," I said. "And if we were back in the cottage at Penzance, with nothing worse to fight than mosquitoes —"

We had no midday meal, but at dusk Tish was lucky enough to capture a knapsack set down by a German soldier just outside the machine-gun aperture, and we ate what I believe are termed emergency rations. By that time it was quite dark, and Tish announced that the time had come to strike, though she refused any other explanation.

We had no difficulty in getting out of the cellar, and Tish led the way immediately to the foot of the tower.

"We must get rid of the sentry up there," she whispered. "The moment he hears a racket in the street he will signal for reënforcements, which would be unfortunate."

"What racket?" I demanded.

But she did not reply. Instead she moved into the recess below the tower and stood looking up thoughtfully. I joined her, and we could make out what seemed to be a platform above, and we distinctly saw a light on it, as though the lookout had struck a match. I suggested firing up at him, but Tish sniffed.

"And bring in the entire regiment, or whatever it is!" she said scornfully but in a whisper. "Use your brains, Lizzie!"

However, at that moment the sentry solved the question himself, for he started down. We could hear his coming. We concealed ourselves hastily, and Tish watched him go out and into a cellar across the street, where she said she was convinced they were serving beer. Indeed, there could be no doubt of it, she maintained, as the men went there in crowds, and many of them carried tin cups.

Tish's first thought was that he would be immediately relieved by another lookout, and she stationed herself inside the door, ready to make him prisoner. But finally the truth dawned on us that he had temporarily deserted his post. Tish took immediate advantage of his absence to prepare to ascend the tower, and having found a large knife in the knapsack she had salvaged she took it between her teeth and climbed the narrow winding staircase.

"If he comes back before I return, Lizzie," she said, "capture him, but don't shoot. It might make the rest suspicious."

She then disappeared and I heard her climbing the stairs with her usual agility. However, she returned considerably sooner than I had anticipated, and in a state of intense anger.

"There is another one up there," she whispered. "I heard him sneezing. Why he didn't shoot at me I don't know, unless he thought I was the other one. But I've fixed him," she added with a tinge of complacency. "It's a rope ladder at the top. I reached up as high as I could and cut it."

She then grew thoughtful and observed that cutting the

ladder necessitated changing a part of her plan.

"What plan?" I demanded. "I guess my life's at stake as well as yours, Tish Carberry."

"I should think it would be perfectly clear," she said. "We've either got to take this town or starve like rats in that cellar. They've got so now that they won't even walk on the side next to the church, and some of them cross themselves. The frying pan seems to have started it, and when the knapsack disappeared — However, here's my plan, Lizzie. From what I have observed during the day pretty nearly the entire lot, except the sentries, will be in that beer cellar across in an hour or so. The rest will run for it — take my word — the moment I open fire."

"I'll take your word, Tish," I said. "But what if they don't run?"

She merely waved her hand.

"My plan is simply this," she said: "I've been tinkering with that machine gun most of the day, and my conviction is that it will work. You simply turn a handle like a hand sewing machine. As soon as you hear me starting it you leave the church by that shell hole at the back and go as rapidly as possible back to the American lines. I'll guarantee," she added grimly, "that not a German leaves that cellar across the street until my arm's worn out."

"What shall I say, Tish?" I quavered.

I shall never forget the way she drew herself up.

"Say," she directed, "that we have captured the town of V — and that they can come over and plant the flag."

I must profess to a certain anxiety during the period of waiting that followed. I felt keenly the necessity of leaving my dear Tish to capture and hold the town alone. And various painful thoughts of Aggie added to my uneasiness. Nor was my perturbation decreased by the reëntrance of the lookout some half hour after he had gone out. Concealed behind debris we listened to his footsteps as he ascended the tower, and could distinctly hear his ferocious mutterings when he discovered that the rope had been cut.

But strangely enough he did not call to the other man, cut off on the platform above.

"I don't believe there was another," I whispered to Tish. But she was confident that she had heard one, and she observed that very probably the two had quarreled.

"It is a well-known tendency of two men, cut off from their kind," she said, "to become violently embittered toward each other. Listen. He is coming down."

I regret to say that he raised an immediate alarm, and that we were forced to retire behind our sarcophagus in the cellar for some time. During the search the enemy was close to us a number of times, and had not one of them stepped on the nail which had served us so usefully I fear to think what might have happened. He did so, however, and retired snarling and limping.

I believe Tish has given nine o'clock in her report to G. H. Q. as the time when she opened fire. It was therefore about eight forty-five when I left the church. For some time before that the cellar across had been filling up with the enemy, and the search for us had ceased. By Tish's instructions I kept to back ways, throwing a grenade here and there to indicate that the attack was a strong one, and also firing my revolver. On hearing the firing behind them the Germans in the advanced trenches apparently considered that they had been cut off from the rear, and I understand that practically all of them ran across to our lines and surrendered. Indeed I was almost run down by three of them.

I was almost entirely out of breath when I reached our trenches, and had I not had the presence of mind to shout "Kamerad," which I had heard was the customary thing, I dare say I should have been shot.

I remember that as I reached the trenches a soldier called out: "Damned if the whole German Army isn't surrendering!"

I then fell into the trench and was immediately caught in a very rude manner. When I insisted that he let me go the man who had captured me only yelled when I spoke, and dropped his gun.

"Hey!" he called. "Fellows! Come here! The boches have taken to fighting their women."

"Don't be a fool!" I snapped. "We've taken V — , and I must see the commanding officer at once."

"You don't happen to have it in your pocket, lady, have you?" he said. He then turned a light on me and said: "Holy mackerel! It's Miss Lizzie! What's this about V —?"

"Miss Carberry has taken V — ," I said.

"I believe you," was all he said; and we started for headquarters.

I recall distinctly the scene in the general's headquarters when we got there. The general was sitting, and both Charlie Sands and Mr. Burton were there, looking worried and unhappy. At first they did not see me, and I was too much out of breath to speak.

"I have already told you both that I cannot be responsible for three erratic spinsters. They are undoubtedly prisoners if they returned to V — ."

"Prisoners!" said Charlie Sands. "If they were prisoners would they be signaling from the church tower for help?"

"I have already heard that story. It's ridiculous. Do you mean to tell me that with that town full of Germans those women have held the church tower since last night?"

Mr. Burton drew a piece of paper from his pocket.

"From eight o'clock to nine," he said, "the signal was 'Help,' repeated at frequent intervals; shortly after nine there was an attempt at a connected message. Allowing for corrections and for the fact that the light was growing dim, as though from an over-used battery, the message runs: 'Help. Bring a ladder. They have cut the —' I am sorry that the light gave out just there, and the message was uncompleted."

How terrible were my emotions at that time, to think that our dear Tish had cut off Aggie's only hope of escape.

The general got up.

"I am, afraid you young gentlemen are indulging in a sense of humor at my expense. Unfortunately I have no sense of humor, but you may find it funny. Captain Sands to continue under arrest for last night's escapade. As Mr. Burton is a member of a welfare organization I do not find him under my direct jurisdiction, but —"

"Then I shall go to V — myself!" Mr. Burton said angrily. "I'll capture the whole damned town single-handed, and —"

I then entered the cellar and said: "Miss Carberry has captured V — , general. She asks me to tell you that you may come over at any time and plant the flag. The signaling is being done by Miss Pilkington, who is at present holding the tower. I am acting as runner."

I regret to say that I cannot publish the general's reply.

As the remainder of the incident is a matter of historical record I shall not describe the advance of a portion of our Army into V — .

They found the garrison either surrendered, fled or under Tish's fire in the beer cellar, and were, I believe, at first seriously menaced by that indomitable figure. It was also extremely difficult to rescue Aggie, as at first she persisted in firing through the floor of the platform the moment she heard any one ascending. In due time, however, she was brought down, but as any mention of the tower for some time gave her a nervous chill it was several weeks before we heard her story.

I doubt if we would have heard it even then had not Mr. Burton and Hilda come to Paris on their wedding trip. We had a dinner for them at the Café de Paris, and Mr. Burton told us that we were all to have the Croix de Guerre. He insisted on ordering champagne to celebrate, and Aggie had two glasses, and then said the room was going round like the weather vane on the tower at V —.

She then went rather white and said: "The ladder was fastened to it, you know."

"What ladder?" Tish asked sharply.

"The rope ladder I was standing on. And when the wind blew —"

Well, we gave her another glass of wine, and she told us the tragic story. She had fallen behind me, and was round a corner, when she felt a sneezing spell coming on. So seeing a doorway she slipped in, and she sneezed for about five minutes. When she came out there was nobody in sight, and after wandering round she went back to the doorway and closed the door.

There were stairs behind her, and when the counter attack came she ran up the stairs. She knew then that she was in the church tower, but she didn't dare to come down. When the firing stopped in the streets a soldier ran down the stairs and almost touched her. A moment later she heard him coming back, so she climbed up ahead and got out on a balcony above the clock. But he started to come out on the balcony, and just as she was prepared to be shot her hand touched a rope ladder and she went up it like a shot.

"It was dark, Tish," she said with a shudder, "and I couldn't look down. But when morning came I was up beside the weather vane, and a sniper from our lines must have thought I didn't belong there, for he fired at me every now and then."

Well, it seems she hung there all day, and nobody noticed her. Luckily the wind mostly kept her from the German side, and the sentry couldn't see her from the balcony. Then at last, the next evening, she heard him going down, and she would have made her escape, but he had cut the rope ladder below. She couldn't imagine why.

Tish looked at me steadily.

"It is very strange," she said. "But who can account for the instinct of destruction in the Hun mind?"

THE END